My Brother's Keeper

My Brother's Keeper

This novel is a work of fiction. Any references to real people, events, establishments, or locales are intended only to give the fiction a sense of reality and authenticity. Other names, characters, and incidents occurring in the work are either the product of the author's imagination or are used fictitiously, as those fictionalized events and incidents that involve real persons. Any character that happens to share the name of a person who is an acquaintance of the author, past or present, is purely coincidental and is in no way intended to be an actual account involving that person.

ISBN- 13: 978-1481297882
ISBN- 10: 1481297880
LCCN: 2014900765

First Printing January 2012

Printed in the United States of America

Cover Design by Kyeon Trevon

My Brother's Keerper

Jade Jones

Wisdom

1991

Gazing at the small, dark blemish on Imani's left breast, I ran my fingers through her tussled hair as she slept. She had burned herself there a few weeks ago while flat ironing her hair shirtless. She stirred but remained asleep and I took that as an opportunity to brush a gentle kiss over the sexy mark she'd been left with. I loved every inch and everything about this girl. Even her imperfections.

Smiling at myself, I thought about how my boys back at home would be clowning me if they knew how whipped I was over this girl.

She stirred softly before revealing a set of beautiful hazel eyes. "You were watching me sleeping?" she mumbled. Her full and luscious lips formed into a sexy smirk.

I leaned down and kissed her forehead. "I always do," I whispered.

She covered her face with her hands. "Oh, why do you do that? I bet I look ridiculous."

I slowly removed her hands. "You don't look ridiculous," I assured her. "But you do make some funny faces," I quickly added.

She shoved me playfully. "Whatever, Wisdom."

I looked down into her beautiful face, taking in all of her features. Imani had the smoothest brown skin. She was a petite girl, standing at a mere five foot two inches, but she had just enough assets in all the right places. Her long reddish-brown hair was thick and natural. But I'd have to say her lips were her most beautiful feature. Plump and pouty.

I leaned over and kissed her delectable lips once more, before settling down beside her. She ran her fingers through my short curly hair, a habit of hers.

During the spur of the moment, my eyes wandered over towards the framed picture on my nightstand. June 6, 1989. Graduation day. Wearing a navy blue cap and gown with a smile from ear to ear, I would have to say that was the proudest day of my life. My twin brother, Chance (who was dressed in casual attire) had one arm casually slung over my shoulder while he threw the peace sign up with his other. Uncle Lou was to my left and Aunt May was standing beside Chance, holding up my High School diploma. I had obtained a 4.3 GPA and an SAT score of 2300 upon graduating at the age of seventeen. My mother would have been so proud of me.

Kimberly Ainesworthe had singlehandedly raised me and Chance. We had never met our father, and the only thing we knew about him was that he was a happily married white man who wanted nothing to do with us. He had abandoned his sons before we were born. But you can't miss what you never had, right? I was fine without a so-called "father figure". Chance, on the other hand...he might have needed that father figure more than he cared to acknowledge.

While I was the only one of us with my my head in the books, Chance, however, found affinity running the streets. And after our mother was murdered, things only went downhill for him.

Suddenly, Imani began pulling the sheets from her body.

"Yo, where're you going?" I asked.

"I told you. I have my African American studies class today," she said looking over at the digital alarm clock. It read 11:04 a.m.

I pinched an erect dark brown nipple. "That class can't wait?" I bit my lip, anticipating a second round.

"Now, Wisdom, you know I can't afford to miss class," she said matter-of-factly.

"But this is the last day of school," I whined.

Imani climbed out of bed, and began pulling on a pair of form fitting stone wash jeans."It's not the last day of school. It's only Spring break," she said.

In admiration, I watched her bare breasts bounce while she tried to pull the jeans over her hips.

"When we get back, I'll have a whole slew of work," she explained as she pulled on a gray one shoulder sweater.

I licked my lips, eased the sheets below my waist to expose my excitement. "I like that word...slew."

Imani burst into laughter. "Oh, you like that word, huh?"

Flexing my dick, I told her, "Yeah, why don't you come slew this."

She tried her best to ignore my outlandish act. "Boy, you aren't even using the word the right way."

I smiled. "In my head I am."

She placed her hands on her hips. "Oh yeah? And which head is that?"

I chuckled and slid the sheets back over my stiff one. Her bourgeoisie ass parents were paying out of pocket for her to attend Harvard, so I knew the real reason why she couldn't afford to miss class.

I, however, was a bit more fortunate, coming from a low income family. Uncle Lou and Aunt May couldn't possibly afford to send me to school. Hell, they barely could afford to adopt me and Chance after moms passed away. Aunt May was my mother's older sister, she had a heart of gold. She took my brother and I in without so much as a second thought, even though Uncle Lou was a little hesitant at first. Although my aunt and uncle had no children, they treated me and Chance as if we were their own. "

Are you going to meet me in the study room after class?" she asked.

"Why don't you just come back to my dorm?" I asked eagerly.

She smirked. "Your room mate will be here by then."

"Well, why can't I meet you in your dorm?"

She smiled. "My roommate will be there, baby." She walked over and sat on the edge of my bed. "You know how uncomfortable she gets when you come around."

I couldn't help but to sigh, knowing I wouldn't be hitting that anytime soon. Her stuck up roommate was intimidated by anyone with a tint of color in their skin.

"Yeah, I guess so. Can't leave without saying my goodbye to you," I said with purpose.

Imani playfully shoved me. "Come on now, knock it off. You know you're more than welcome to visit me anytime at home. You always have an invite."

I sucked my teeth. "Yo, your parents tense up worst around me than your damn roommate."

Imani insisted on lying to me about her parents liking me, but it didn't take a rocket scientist to see otherwise. I could see the disappointment all over her father's face the minute she introduced us. You would've thought by me being an Honor student enrolled in an Ivy League college, I would have impressed him. After all there were only a handful of black students enrolled in such a prestigious school. Whether it was the baggy clothes or casual tone, his unmistakable disdain for me was obvious. Imani had never met my family but I knew for a fact that they'd welcome her with open arms. They were tight like that.

"My parents love you," she lied. "And so do I," she added before planting a kiss on my forehead.

"Love you too."

She stood up. "Well, let me get going before I'm late." And just like that I watched her sexy ass leave my dorm.

After showering and dressing I headed down to the study room. I tried to read my copy of Ebony Magazine but I quickly found myself unable to focus on an article about Thurgood Marshall. My mind kept shifting home. For an entire year I had easily avoiding returning home during school breaks. And it wasn't because I didn't miss my aunt and uncle. The fact of the matter was, I was avoiding Chance. See, Chance had this problem where he would habitually drag me into his bullshit. Any situation he found himself in, usually ended up with me somehow involved.

Now that I was in college, I guess it was safe to say that I wanted no part of whatever nonsense he associated himself with. I couldn't afford to sacrifice my education and future. So I did what I had to do. I stayed away. Realizing I stayed out of trouble as long as I stayed away from my brother.

"Where is she?" I asked myself, looking around the study room. Two hours had quickly elapsed and there was still no sign of Imani. Her A.A. Studies class lasted only an hour and fifteen minutes.

I rolled up the magazine and stuffed in the back pocket of my jeans before heading upstairs to Imani's dormitory. Once I reached her room, I discovered her door slightly ajar. She was sitting on the edge of her bed with her back turned to me.

"Mani?"

She didn't respond.

I walked over to her and took a seat beside her. In her left hand was her Motorola brick phone, and in her right hand was a single Kleenex tissue. "My mom just called," she said. "Her and daddy are going out of town together for Spring break, so they won't be coming to get me." She sniffled. "You'd think they..." She let her voice trail off. She turned to face me, tears in her eyes. "I guess I'll be staying here in Cambridge." She gave a weak smile.

I wiped away at an oncoming tear. "I'll stay here with you," I told her. And I honestly wouldn't mind it at all.

"No, you've already told your family you'll be coming home. They're expecting you. They haven't seen you in a while"--

"Yo, check this out. Why don't you come home with me? You could spend the break with me and my family. You're always saying how you want to meet my aunt and uncle.

Imani remained silent as she mulled it over for a second. "I can't," she finally said.

"Why can't you?" I asked. "My peoples are cool. They won't mind." Truthfully I didn't know if they'd mind or not. "Would you really rather stay here?"

She thought about it once more. "You're sure they won't mind?"

"Yes, I'm sure. They won't mind at all." I reassured her. "They're mad cool. You'll see."

After much deliberation she finally threw her arms around my neck and kissed me. "Thank you," she smiled.

"Come on. Start packing. They're expecting me around seven. And my aunt said she's cooking." I told her, "You haven't had real food until you had a home cooked meal by Aunt May."

Wisdom

I was born and raised in Philadelphia. North Philly to be exact. I knew my city like the back of my hand and loved my hood. But I'd be lying if I said I didn't like the fact that I stayed six hours away. Honestly, living on campus kept me out of the trouble I was bound to be in had I stayed home.

After pulling up to the curb in front of my aunt and uncle's brick red row home, I looked over at Imani. She was fast asleep with her seat reclined back and her bare feet propped above the glove compartment box.

I reached over and softly nudged her shoulder. "Yo, wake up babe. We're here."

The minute she opened her eyes I noticed the sudden apprehension.

I doubted she was nervous about meeting my family. Imani was born and raised in Potomac, Maryland. Her father was a well=known and successful jazz record producer while her mother was a high profile lawyer. She was born into wealth. Raised in a rich town with huge houses, private schools, and an up-scale environment, she had probably only seen the ghetto on television.

North Philly had been labeled as a high crime, poverty-stricken drug zone. But I had never looked at it that way. People were only trying to get by. Eat. Survive. This was my hood, so I took the good with the bad and made the best of it.

"This is where you live?" Imani asked, taking in her surroundings. Across the street were a couple of little girls jump roping, paying no mind to the passing wino drinking a forty ounce wrapped in a brown paper bag.

Sitting on the porch steps of a house, drinking cans and beer, and sharing a single blunt were a few of the guys I recognized from the hood. Nothing out of the ordinary.

"Yes, ma'am," I answered.

Imani tried her best to relax. "Glad we're finally here. My butt is killing me," she smiled.

I hit the door unlock button. "I can make it feel better."

"Yeah, I just bet you can," she laughed as she closed the door behind her.

I hadn't even reached my house's cracked stone steps before Chance came rushing through the screen door.

"Yo, whuddup college boy!" he hollered, throwing his arms in the air.

I must admit I was happy as hell to see him. Even though he kept me in a lot of shit, I missed his crazy ass. "Whuddup, bro!"

He skipped down the cracked steps and embraced me in a brotherly hug.

"Yo, that's that nigga, Wiz! Whuddup boy!" That was one of the guys sitting on the steps.

I waved at Johnny, who had been Chance's homeboy since middle school.

"Long time no see, nigga!" he hollered down the row of houses.

"Man, too long. Damn, I see you got on the new Jays. You gonna let me borrow them jawns?" he asked. "Look at you boy! Look like you put on weight too. College feeding your ass good too, huh, motherfucker?"

I burst into laughter and patted my abs. His mind was playing tricks on him.

"Chance, I know that ain't your behind cursing like that?" Aunt May hollered as she approached the screen door. The moment she saw me she gasped and placed her hand over her chest. "You're here," she said breathlessly. Aunt May looked like a heavier version of my mother. Her hair was always in a set of rollers as if that were a hairstyle itself.

Aunt May quickly came outside playfully shoving Chance out of her way. "Come here, come here. Let me take a look at my baby." She quickly looked me over before pulling me into a bear hug. "I missed you so much. And I'm proud of you, baby."

"I missed you too, Aunt May."

When she finally released me, I was surprised to see tears welling up. However, I knew the sentiment was anything but sad. Soon after, Uncle Lou came limping out onto the porch.

"Bout time," he joked. "Well, don't stand there. Come give me some love."

Uncle Lou was a tall, slender, dark skinned man. He was born with Polio but that never seemed to stop him from kicking me and Chance's ass when we were younger.

"Come on now, Unc," I laughed as we hugged each other.

Imani began shuffling from one foot to the other, perhaps irritated that I had not introduced her yet. I walked over to her. "Chance...Aunt May, Uncle Lou...this is my girlfriend, Imani." I said putting my arm around her.

Chance wet his lips, Aunt May's eyebrows raised, and Uncle Lou remained expressionless.

"I told her she could stay here with me for Spring Break," I continued.

Chance looked over at Aunt may, who's mouth was wide open. Uncle Lou twisted his face up.

"Oh, well, okay. Sure," Aunt May said after several seconds. "Any friend of Wisdom's is a friend of the family's."

Chance sucked his teeth. "Aunt May, how come you never felt that way about Johnny?"

She looked over in Johnny's direction, who was now entertaining the fellas on the steps. Evidently he thought he looked cool moon walking in house shoes with a can of beer in one hand.

"Boy, please," she spat. "Now help your brother with his bags. Oh, Wisdom, I'm so glad you're home. I cooked a little meal. Are you two hungry?" She looked at Imani specifically.

"I'm starving," Imani smiled.

"Oh, well you're in for quite a treat young lady." she said. "And I made your favorite, Wisdom. Peach cobbler for dessert."

"Hey, Aunt May, can I come get a plate?" Johnny yelled, obviously eavesdropping.

"Boy, you come down here, you gone get more than a plate," Uncle Lou threatened, holding up his cane.

Wisdom

Fried chicken, collard greens, six cheese macaroni, dressing, and cornbread was the little meal Aunt May had prepared.

"Aunt May, you went out your way," I said after we were all seated at the dining room table. "You didn't have to do all this for me."

"Nonsense," she said. "I wanted to cook a nice dinner. It's been a while since we all sat down and ate dinner together like a family."

"Yeah, nigga. You needed some soul food. I know your ass was up there eating crackers and plants and shit, like them white folks!" Chance began laughing at his own crude humor, and I even caught Imani trying to stifle a giggle.

"Chance, hush up!" Aunt May hissed. "Now everybody hold hands so we can say grace." Every one held hands and bowed their heads. "Lord, I would like to thank you for blessing this family, and reuniting us tonight so that we may enjoy this meal. Dear God, I am truly thankful for you watching over both of my nephews. Please continue to bless this household, bless our friends and family, and even bless our enemies. In Jesus' name, I pray. Amen."

"Amen," we chanted in unison.

"Let's eat," Uncle Lou smiled.

You would've thought it was Thanksgiving by the way we each piled our plates.

"So, um....Imani...that's your name, right?" Chance asked.

Imani smiled as she forked some collard greens and neck bones onto her plate."That's correct."

"So, um...how long you and my brother been together?"

I cut my eyes over at Chance. I knew where this was going before it even began.

"We've, uh, been dating for about eight or nine months now."

"How old are you?" he quickly asked.

"Yo, Chance. Come on now," I spoke up. "Can't you save the questions until after we eat?"

Imani spoke up. "No, it's quite okay. I don't mind his inquisitiveness."

Chance smiled. "Yeah, bro. She don't mind my inquisitiveness," he mocked.

"I just turned twenty last month," Imani answered.

"Oh, so you're a year older than my brother." He raised an eyebrow. "An older girl."

Imani smiled. "That I am."

"So what are you in school for?" Aunt May suddenly asked.

First Chance. Now Aunt May.

"My major is Afro American black studies. This is my third year. I'd like to become a professor someday."

Chance smiled mischievously. "A professor, huh?"

"Yes. I've always loved the idea of teaching."

"What about you?" Uncle Lou interjected. "You found yourself a major yet?"

"I'm still undecided," I admitted shamefully. I was hoping they'd change the subject from school to something else. I was miles away from Harvard but it still managed to dominate a conversation.

"Yo, if you don't mind me asking, what is your race?" Chance foolishly asked. "I mean., you have this unique look to you. You Rican?"

Imani furrowed her brow. She was so cute when she did that. "I look different?" she repeated.

"Well, yeah."

I cut my eyes at Chance.

"Wow." she smiled. "Well, I'll take that as a compliment. I like different."

"You can't blame me for asking." he said, looking at me in particular. "You might be my future sister-in-law. I want to know everything about you. It ain't everyday Wiz brings home a beautiful girl. I mean, he was never much of a ladies man like me and shit."

Uncle Lou choked back his laughter. Aunt May rolled her eyes. This conversation was irritating me.

"Well, um..." she tried to hold back her laughter. "I'm not Puerto-Rican, but I will say that is the first time I've heard that." she said. "No, um, actually my father is African. My mother is Irish and French. I guess I'm a bit of a mutt." she smiled.

Chance scrutinized her from across the table and I wished I was close enough to kick his ass in the shin.

"Aunt May, let me get the dishes for you." I offered, feeling a little guilty about her cleaning up behind everyone.

"Oh, sweetie, thanks. But I can manage. You just get Imani settled in. She seems like a sweet girl."

I joined her at the kitchen sink and proceeded to place the clean dishes into the dish rack. "Yeah, she's a good girl. Focused. Motivated. That's why I'm with her."

"I wish Chance had as good as taste in women as you. You know he's got some floozy showing up here at all times of the day harassing us. Telling everybody she just had his baby. Girl's a mess."

I raised an eyebrow in skepticism. "Word?" Shaking my head, I asked her, "So how's everything been with you?"

Aunt May exhaled deeply. Obviously something was on her mind. "Well," she sighed. "Last week I had to go to the hospital. Blood pressure was sky high." she explained. "Doctor says I'm stressed."

"You sure it's not the food," I joked. "You know soul food is killing us black folks."

Aunt May chuckled. "They teach you that in Harvard?"

I snickered. "No."

Aunt May quickly shifted her mood to a more serious one. "I've been worried about Chance." She sighed. "Twice last month we had to bail his butt out of jail for silly crap. He's getting worse, Wisdom. He's out here running the streets day and night. I'm afraid something bad is going to happen to him." She spoke with urgency. "And I won't be able to bail him out of the grave." she commented. "Honestly, I was hoping you could talk some sense into him while you're here, you know? Maybe a pep talk. Brother to brother."

Chance was bullheaded. He hated any type of advice or opinions. Especially if it was for his own benefit. Instead of telling my aunt what she already knew, I said, "Don't worry Aunt May. I'll talk to him."

She leaned over and kissed my cheek. "Thanks, baby. I'm so glad you're home."

I decided to change the subject. "So did you get the money I sent you?"

Aunt May rolled her eyes. "Yes, I got it. But I wish you would stop sending me your grant money.We're fine here. You use that money for your books and things."

"I just feel like I owe you. I mean, without you putting me in that private high school, I"--

"Wisdom, you don't owe me a thing. Let's get that clear," she said. "I took the steps I needed to take because I knew you had a bright future ahead of you. Your mother would've did the same thing," she explained. "So don't ever feel like you owe me anything, because you graduating and going to college is the greatest way you could ever repay me." She smiled. "Now I wish I could say the same about your knucklehead brother in there."

I found Chance in the living room, showing Imani old photographs from when we were kids.

"Yeah, that's Wisdom's old snot nose ass." he said pointing to the picture.

"Oh, my God," she covered her mouth to keep from laughing. "You were so cute with your little cut up jeans," she lied.

I sucked my teeth. "Yo, let me see that."

Imani stifled a giggle as she handed me the photo album. I looked over the old, faded picture of me and Chance. I was wearing a blue and orange striped rugby shirt and green shorts. Chance had on a black t-shirt, frayed jeans, and a red and white baseball cap.

"Fool, that's you with that snotty ass nose!"

"I'm amazed that you two can even tell each other apart on pictures. I mean, you two are identical!" She looked at Chance then back at me. "I can't spot a single thing that would help me to tell you apart."

"When he opens his mouth, you'll be able to tell us apart," I joked.

"Yo, you ain't even been here a whole day, and you already cracking on a nigga."

The abrupt banging on the screen door interrupted us.

"Yo, who dat?" Chance hollered, walking over to the front door. "Bitch nigga, don't be coming to the crib banging on doors and shit like you five-oh or something!"

"Come on, bay. Let me get you settled in," I told Imani.

<u>Chance</u>

"Whuddup, mark ass."

"Whuddup fool," Johnny gave me dap. "Yo, I been casing that joint up there in Chestnut Hill."

"Word?"

Johhny took a long drag on the blunt encased between his two fingers. "Motherfuckers finally took dat trip."

"Yo, pass that jawn."

Johnny took another drag before handing me the blunt.

He had been my homeboy before puberty kicked in on both our asses. And he had been sporting that same silly ass "gumby haircut" since he was twelve. He was a goofball most of the time but he was serious when it came to making money. And that's the primary reason why I fucked with him. Johnny didn't give a damn how he earned his money as long as he did.

Johnny fixed his mouth up to say something, but quickly stopped the minute he saw Wisdom appear at the screen door. We knew better than to discuss certain things in front of him. I loved my brother, but sometimes he could be so fucking judgmental.

Yo, I'll meet you down at your place," I told Johnny.

"Cool, but can I get my shit back, though?" he asked, holding his hand out.

I laughed. "Nigga, fuck you! My joint now."

He shook his head as he turned and headed back to his house.

"Can I talk to you for a second?" Wisdom asked, stepping out onto the porch.

Here we go, I thought as I took another drag on the blunt. "What's up?"

"What's been up with you, man?" he asked.

I shrugged. "Same shit. Nothing new. Hell, you know me."

His jaw tensed as he looked me over, trying to read me. I hated when he did that shit. Just because we were identical twins didn't mean he could read my fucking mind.

"You working?" he asked.

I exhaled deeply. "Come on now nigga. I ain't got time to be standing behind some fryer. I got better ways to get money."

"With Johnny?" Wisdom retorted.

I immediately wondered just how much of my conversation he had heard. He always was a sneaky motherfucker.

"I get my money. You don't need to know the details," I retaliated. Hell, this nigga hadn't even been here a whole day yet and he was already trippin' on me.

"Well, Aunt May has been worried about the details. She said she had to bail you out twice last month—"

"She tell you to come out here and talk to me?"

He ignored my question. "You know she had to go to the hospital two weeks ago?" Wisdom asked.

"Yeah, 'cause of her blood pressure"--

"No, because of you!" Wisdom snapped. "Chance, she's all we got, man. Her and Uncle Lou. If you cared about her half as much as you care about yourself you would be a little considerate, bro'. She's older now, and we ain't kids no more," he explained. "She ain't got time to be chasing your ass in the streets. Why don't you get a job and—"

"And be like you?" I retorted.

Wisdom sighed.

"That's what you were going to say, right, college boy?" I asked. "I should be more like you?"

Wisdom and I stared at each other in silence for several seconds.

"Well, motherfucker, I'm not like you. When you gonna understand that? Process that shit!"

"Chance—"

"I don't need you coming out here trying to give me no bullshit ass pep talk. You're my brother! Not my fucking father! So cut the act already." I told him. "You know I'm gonna do me no matter who likes it. I'm not you, aight? So you and Aunt May need to get that through ya'll heads."

"Chance, are you going to let me talk?" he asked.

I flicked the butt of the joint on the ground, and didn't look at him when I said, "Naw. I'm done talking." And with that I turned my back on him and headed to Johnny's crib.

***

Johnny was bumping N.W.A.'s "100 Miles and Running" when he eased his '86 Corolla to a slow stop. He parked directly across the street from the home we were preparing to case. We'd been breaking into houses together since we were thirteen. We were now vets at this shit.

"Yo, why the fuck is a light on upstairs?" I asked, easing on a pair of black leather gloves.

Johnny killed the engine. "Motherfuckers are trying to make it look like they're home. Trust me that joint is empty as hell," he assured me.

I grabbed the gray duffel bag from the back seat. It contained every essential item needed to case a home. We sat in the car for fifteen minutes, until we were certain there weren't any nosy ass neighbors in sight. Once we were satisfied we crept out of the car and headed over to the home.

I followed Johnny to the side of the house. "These motherfuckers usually leave this window open." He began yanking on the window but it wouldn't budge.

"Yeah, genius, looks like they locked it, since they went out of town, right?" I joked.

"Man just hand me the crowbar."

He quickly and efficiently broke the upper right corner of the window. It wasn't too noisy but I still looked around to make sure no one's lights came on.

Johnny slipped his hand inside the window and unlocked it.

"Yo, hurry up," I urged.

He quickly yanked the window up and climbed in. I followed suite, but unfortunately ended up tripping on the way in, landing right on my ass.

Johnny found that shit hilarious.

"Yo, turn the damn light on."

Once he flicked the light switch on, I noticed we were in the kitchen. I walked over to the fridge and looked at the calendar on it. Sure enough it was marked that the family would be in Florida for an entire week.

"What the fuck are you doing?" Johnny asked laughing.

I pulled a red apple from the fridge, walked over to the sink, and rinsed it off. "What? I got the munchies."

"Aye, check this shit out," Johnny said, picking up a bottle of wine from the kitchen counter. "Moscato 1964. Looks like they forgot to celebrate."

"Pass that jawn. Shit we can celebrate right now."

Fifteen minutes after popping the cork, the bottle was empty. Rummaging through the entire house, we had collected jewelry, tools, a Gameboy, and a Sega Genesis. Finding the Smith & Wesson stainless steel pistol was a bonus. Neither of us found cash, but after we pawned everything we'd definitely have a little money in our pockets.

We stayed thirty minutes over our usual time limit, but we were too fucked up to even notice or care about duration and accuracy.

Once we were back in the car I couldn't help but to reexamine the pistol. I brushed my fingers over the stainless steel. I had never possessed a gun. Just holding it in my hand gave me a weird sense of strength and authority. I didn't know if I was bugging off my buzz, but I really loved the way it felt in my hand.

"Yo, we could get some serious cash for that."

I cut my eyes at Johnny. "Fool, I ain't pawning this. I'm keeping this shit."

"Word?" Johnny asked, peaking over at the gun while driving.

I ignored him as I continued to stroke the barrel of the   gun.

Chance

Johnny and I were cruising along Kensington Avenue underneath the elevated train tracks when something finally caught my eye. "Hold on right quick. Pull over."

Johnny cackled as he eased his car alongside the curb. He must've seen her before I did.

I lowered my window and shouted out, "What's up, mami?"

Wearing a black leather jacket, fishnet stockings, and black knee high boots she strolled over with confidence. "Que pasa, papi. What you looking for?" she asked.

"How much you gonna charge to give me and my home boy some head?" I asked her. She wasn't much to look at. Her face was caked with foundation, her dark

Burgundy lipstick was exaggerated, and you could see the pockmarks on her face a mile away, even with all the makeup poorly concealing them. It didn't matter to me though. I wouldn't have to see her face with her head in my lap.

She smiled revealing a set of yellow tinted teeth. "Forty. And that's a special for you cutie."

I climbed out the car and opened the back door. "Get in."

She didn't hesitate as she climbed into the backseat. "I'll need the money up front, papi."

I climbed into the backseat with her. With a convincing smile I said, "Don't worry mami, I got you. Does it look like I will be on bullshit?"

She smiled. And I wished she would stop doing that shit. "No."

"Okay then." I unbottoned my jeans and slid them down to my knees just as Johnny pulled off.

"Oh, you're big," she whispered, pulling my dick out through the opening of my boxers.

I shoved her face in my lap, shutting her up once and for all. As she went to work devouring me like the professional she was I lit up another joint. I watched in admiration as she went to work, polishing my dick with her mouth. I loved the sounds she made as she sucked me off. Up and down. From tip to base.

"Here it come," I whispered.

She tried to pull her head from my lap, but I grabbed her by the nape of her neck and forced her to stay in that position. She bucked, tried to get out of my vice grip.

"Uh-uh, swallow it. Swallow it." I groaned as I shot my seeds down this hoe's throat.

She made gurgling sounds as if she wanted to vomit but I kept her ass there until I knew she had no choice but to swallow.

"Que diablos? What the fuck is your problem?" she screamed. "I charge extra for that. Pay up," she ordered.

"Naw bitch, you pay up!"

She looked down at the shiny pistol I had aimed at her lower midsection.

"Are you fucking kidding me?" she asked, looking from Johnny back to me.

"Yo, I don't think he's playing," Johnny said.

She sucked her teeth as she un-zipped her leather jacket, dug into her bra, and tossed me a small wad of cash.

I flipped through the bills. "Eighty fucking dollars?" I spat. "Bitch, this all you got?"

She sucked her teeth again. "Yeah."

"You ain't put in no type of work tonight," I said.

"My pimp will be looking for your ass, motherfucker. Believe that."

I reached over her and opened the door.

"You ever tucked and rolled, bitch?"

"What?"

I didn't even give her a moment to think about it as I pushed her ass out the moving car. I watched her roll down the street like Michael Jackson during the Pepsi commercial.

Johnny found that shit hilarious.

Wisdom

I flicked my tongue across Imani's left nipple. She arched her back and moaned softly. I kissed her and suckled her bottom lip. P.M. Dawn's "Set Adrift on Memory Bliss" was playing softly in the background.

"Baby, this feels so weird," she whispered.

"Why's that?" I asked, placing soft, placid kisses along her neck.

"I feel bad doing this in your aunt and uncle's house. I mean, they invited me here with open arms. I just feel...bad." she whispered.

She would feel even worse knowing this wasn't my first time sexing a girl in this very bed under my aunt and uncle's noses. But what she didn't know wouldn't hurt her.

I rolled over onto my back and pulled her on top of me. She straddled me without complaint. "We'll be very quiet," I whispered as I palmed her tiny breasts.

The sudden creaking of the bedroom door caused both of our heads to turn in its direction. Strangely, the door was now slightly ajar. Imani jumped off me and covered her naked body with the sheets.

"I know I closed that door," I said, climbing out of bed. I peaked into the hallway and looked around. Empty. After closing my bedroom door again, I told her, "Okay, its closed". Her cheeks were now flushed with embarrassment. She was so modest. "Now back to what we were doing."

"Wisdom, I really feel uncomfortable now." Imani whispered, pulling the sheets tighter around her bosom. I can't say I didn't expect it.

"Okay. Maybe we'll finish another time." I sat on the edge of the bed, disappointed.

She scooted closer to me and kissed my ear. "Maybe another time can be tonight when everyone's asleep," she whispered.

I turned to look her dead in the eye and smiled. "Now that's what I'm talking about." I kissed her on the lips.

After showering and dressing, I decided to drop by Chance's room. I made sure to knock on his bedroom door before entering. He was very serious about that. It was eleven in the morning and he was bumping Public Enemy's "Fight the Power."

I knocked harder, knowing he couldn't possibly hear me over the loud music. Two minutes later there was still no answer. Eventually I let myself in, catching a glimpse of something shiny he quickly shoved underneath his pillow. He jumped out of bed and turned down the volume on his boom box.

"Yo, man you can't knock!" he yelled.

"I did. Maybe if you didn't play your music so loud you could hear me."

"Nigga, that wasn't music." he said. "That was art." he retrieved the blunt that had been tucked behind his ear and placed it in his mouth. "What you want anyway?"

I exhaled deeply. "I, um, I wanted to apologize about last night. I wasn't trying to make you feel like I was coming down on you."

Chance removed the blunt from his lips, and stared at me in astonishment. "Boy, college then made your ass soft."

I crossed my arms. "How's that?"

He laughed. "Yo, I'm fucking with you. It's all good in the hood."

I wanted to ask him if he had been lurking around my bedroom, but I decided against it. Less conflict was better. Instead of interrogating him I decided to join my aunt in the kitchen.

"Good morning, Aunt May," I gave her a kiss on the cheek, while she was flipping a pancake.

"Morning, sweetie. How'd you sleep?"

"I slept great. You need any help?"

"Oh, no, baby"--

Suddenly the sound of a beeping horn outside caught our attention.

"See if that's for us, Wisdom."

I walked over to the kitchen window and peered through the blinds. "I don't know. It's a red car."

Aunt May sighed heavily. "Oh, Lord, it's too early for this. Chance!" she hollered, turning the stove off. "Chance! Get your butt out here!"

"Who's that?" I asked.

"What?" Chance snapped, walking into the kitchen.

"Your little floozy's outside," Aunt May said.

Chance groaned loudly as he walked over to the kitchen window, and peered outside. "Shit," he cursed, storming through the front door. Aunt May and I followed suite.

"Keisha, I told your ass about coming around here!" Chance yelled from the porch.

Keisha put her car in park in the middle of the street and jumped out of it, like she'd lost her damn mind. She rounded the car and put her hands on her hips. Surprisingly, she was a very attractive girl. Keisha was dark skinned, short, and thick in all the right places. Her hair was in finger waves, and her fingernails were four inches long and fire red. She was wearing a black spandex tank top and matching spandex leggings.

Ghetto but sexy.

"I'm tired of playing this fucking game with your ass, Chance!" She screamed, rolling her neck and swaying a long fingernail from right to left. "It's time you took some damn responsibility!"

"Yo, shut that shit up!" Chance yelled.

"No, you step up!" she screamed. "Step up and be a fucking man! If not for me, for your son!"

"Girl, you know that ain't my damn son." Chance waved her off as if she were speaking nonsense. "Quit embarrassing yourself!"

Everyone in the neighborhood was now standing outside to witness the embarrassing scene the two had created. Even Imani and Uncle Lou had stepped out the house to see what all the commotion was.

"Oh, this ain't your fucking son?" she screamed.

Chance laughed at her and said, "Naw."

"Well, I'm glad everyone is out here to witness this shit!" she yelled. She opened the back door of her little red Honda and unfastened the kid in the backseat. With much to prove she hoisted the kid on her hip for all to see. "Look, CJ. Look at your dumb ass daddy!" she spat.

Chance burst into laughter shaking his head at her irate behavior.

Keisha might have been ghetto. She might have been childish. Hell, she might have even been crazy. But the woman was no liar. The kid was the spitting image of Chance. He had high yellow skin, and a curly afro with a grade of hair I knew he couldn't possibly have inherited from his mother. The baby boy looked about nine or ten months old.

"Everybody and anybody with eyes can see this is your fucking baby!"

I looked over at Chance whose expression had momentarily softened. But just as quickly it fluctuated into anger and frustration.

Feeling as if she'd made her point, she finally fastened the baby in his car seat. "Now are we going to talk like adults?" she asked.

He knew that was his baby. He was just too childish to admit it.

"Fuck you, Keisha! That could be any light skin nigga's baby! Everybody in the hood know you's a hoe!"

Keisha threw her hands in her air. "Oh, I'm a hoe now, huh? Was I a hoe when you was eating my pussy the other night?" She screamed the last part so loud I believed the entire Philadelphia had heard.

That immediately sent Chance over the edge seeing as how he leapt off the porch and charged at Keisha full speed. He slapped her with such force, she bounced off her car and fell to the ground.

I jumped off the porch and ran after him. "Yo, man! That's a female!" I screamed. When I reached him I shoved the shit out of his ass. "Aye, man, what the fuck is wrong with you?" I yelled.

His baby's mother was now lying on the ground with a busted nose.

Chance ignored me as he shoved me back twice as hard, nearly causing me to lose my balance.

"So this is the shit you do now?" I yelled. "Go around beating on women?"

"You handle your bitch, I'll handle mine!" he spat.

I didn't think twice when I sent my fist sailing into his jaw. He instantly dropped onto the ground beside his baby's mama. The look on his face was full of shame and embarrassment. The entire block had witnessed me lay his ass out. He stared at me with so much hatred and anguish in his eyes, I almost didn't recognize him.

He picked himself up off the ground and stared at me for several seconds, hands clenched into tight fists. I knew he wanted to hurt me. But instead he pushed past me, bumping his shoulder against mine. I watched as he stormed into the house, slamming the screen door behind him.

"Come on. Get up. Are you okay?" I asked Keisha, helping her up.

"I'm fine," she said, snatching away from me. And without another word she climbed into her little red Honda and sped off.

I turned back around, only to receive the unusual stares from friends and family. In silence I walked back inside the house.

"Wisdom, are you okay?" Imani asked.

I ignored her as I headed in the direction of Chance's bedroom. But to my dismay he was not in there. Hell, he wasn't even in the house for that matter.

"Wisdom, calm down," Aunt May urged. "Just relax."

Chance

The nerve of this nigga, man. I swear if he wasn't my fucking brother I would've pulled that shiny pistol out on his ass. This motherfucker has been gone a whole year and he wants to show up and play mediator. He has no idea what the fuck is going on. I knew a way to fix his ass though. I was so pissed as I stormed up the street away from my house. I could've knocked my brother's block off for the shit he pulled. But instead I decided to use a different tactic to expel my anguish and frustration.

I pulled the stocking mask over my face and stormed into Abduhl's, a convenient store/hoagie shop, located only a few blocks from my home.

"Everybody get on the fucking ground!" I yelled aiming at whoever I saw in sight. A Spanish woman and her son had took to cowering behind the potato chip stand as I pointed the gun at the cashier. "You know what time it is! Empty the fucking drawer!"

The balding Arab stared at me as if he were the one holding the gun in this situation. He obviously had the roles reversed, seeing as how his ass didn't budge.

"Bitch, did you hear me?" I pulled the hammer forward. "I said empty your fucking drawer, motherfucker!" The woman and her son were now crying so loudly that it was breaking my concentration. "Yo, shut the fuck up!" I screamed, turning in my head in their direction--Yet in my peripheral vision I noticed the Arab moving for something beneath the counter. Without deliberation I fired a single shot into his shoulder. My hand instantly jerked at the recoil.

"Arrggghhhh, shit!" he screamed, looking down at the wound, trembling. Beads of sweat had quickly formed on his forehead.

"You made me do it." I yelled, holding the gun with a shaky hand. Little did he know I was just as scared as he was. I had never shot anyone. Sure, I had beat up a couple of guys, sent some fellas to the hospital, and recently pushed a prostitute out of a moving car. But I had never pulled the trigger on someone before.

"Okay, okay," he said. He wasted no time popping open the cash register. With trembling hands he handed me all the money in the drawer.

"Now get on the fucking ground!" I screamed, turning the gun sideways on him. He quickly did as told.

I turned to run out of the store but at the sight of the cowering boy I stopped in my tracks. His mother was holding him tightly, trying to shield his body with hers just in case I decided to pull the trigger on them. For a minute my heart melted as I thought about my mother. She'd be so disappointed in the route I'd chosen to take. Especially a route that ended up being her demise.

Shaking her from my thoughts, I swallowed my dignity and ran out of the store. My mother was dead. She couldn't think, feel, or love any longer.

As I walked into the house, Aunt May asked, "Chance, where have you been?"

"Clearing my mind," I told her.

"Well, do you feel better, honey?" she asked, reaching for my face.

I quickly stopped her from touching me and she drew back at my reaction.

Where's Wisdom?" I asked.

"I had him run to the store to play my number for me," she said. "Are you okay?" she repeated with concern.

Suddenly I felt bad that I was treating my aunt this way. Indeed she was all I had. And no matter how much of a fuck up I was, she was always there for me. Standing in my corner.

I kissed her on the cheek. "Aunt May, I'm fine."

She smiled. "Okay, well get yourself cleaned up. Dinner will be ready soon."

I went to my bedroom, stripped down to my boxers, and headed for the bathroom. Once I reached the closed bathroom door, I pressed my ear up to the door, listening to the soft crooning of a female voice.

Smiling mischievously, I slowly pushed the door open and crept inside. The bathroom was foggy and I could only see the silhouette of Imani's shadow through the drawn pink shower curtains. Quickly pulling my boxers off, I stepped into the shower behind her. She turned around, surprised by my entrance, and I wondered if she truly could tell the difference between me and my brother.

"You scared me," she purred. "Here," she said handing me a blue washcloth. "Could you wash my back for me?" she asked, turning back around.

I took in all of her physique. Imani was sexy as hell. My brother didn't know what to do with her, but I sure did. I could recall when his ass used to be too scared to even approach girls. I used to pretend to be him just to get his ass some play.

Sensually lathering soap over her, I massaged her shoulders while pressing my dick into the cleft of her round ass. She tossed her head back in pleasure and I immediately took that as an opportunity to suck on her neck. She moaned in delight, giving me all the reason I needed to slide a finger into her throbbing pussy from behind. She gyrated her ass on my dick as I finger-fucked her. First one finger. Then two. After several seconds she quickly turned around and pushed me against the wall of the shower.

She jammed her tongue into my mouth as she stroked my dick in her small hand. I grabbed a fistful of her hair and yanked her head back, sucking and licking her neck.

"Not too rough, Wisdom," she moaned.

I ignored her as I bent down and popped a small, brown nipple into my mouth. She quaked and shivered at the way I sucked and chewed on her erect nipple. "Damn, this is a sexy ass birthmark," I whispered.

She quickly pushed me off her. "Wh--What did you say?" she stammered.

I smiled, wet my lips, and said slowly, "This. Is. A. Sexy. Ass. Birthmark." I pinched her nipple, and wasn't surprised when she smacked my hand away. "We already started." I chucked. "Might as well finish."

She quickly climbed out of the shower, and with trembling fingers she wrapped a terry cloth towel around her body. I could tell she was embarrassed by the way I had aroused her.

I turned the shower off, climbed out, and pulled my boxers on. She looked like she'd just seen a ghost as she reached for the door knob--but before she could she open the door, it flung open on its own.

Wisdom looked from Imani, then back at me. His mouth dropped open. And I guessed the wicked smile that crept across my lips sent him over the edge.

"You son of a bitch!" he yelled, tackling me with such force that I hit the back of my head on the edge of the porcelain sink.

Wisdom punched the shit out of me the minute he pinned me down. I felt my lip split open immediately. Before I could react he popped me right in the eye. My face stung as my left eye quickly swelled up.

Using what little strength I could muster up, I flipped him over on his back and punched his ass in the face. Not feeling any type of satisfaction after doing that, I wrapped my hands around his throat. "I hate you, bitch!"

"Enough! Enough of this shit!" Uncle Lou screamed.

I felt like I was flying in the air, when he snatched me off Wisdom. His strength surprised me as he threw me against the hallway wall.

"You two are too damn old to be acting like little kids!" Uncle Lou screamed.

"You are fucked up!" Wisdom screamed in a raspy voice, gripping his throat. "You are so fucked up, Chance!"

"Fuck you!" I screamed.

"You always wanted to be me, chump!" Wisdom yelled. "All our lives you've been jealous of me!"

"Jealous?" I laughed wickedly.

"Yeah, jealous! You heard me motherfucker!"

"What the fuck are you talking about?" I panted.

"You ain't never did shit with your life! And now you're jealous because I did! Yo, you're a fucking failure!" he screamed. "You're a failure as man! You're a failure as a father! You're a failure as a son! You're a failure as nephew! You're a fucking failure as a brother!" he yelled. "You should do yourself a favor and just kill yourself!"

"Wisdom, stop talking like that!" Uncle Lou shouted. "This is your brother. And when me and Aunt May are long gone, you two are going to be all each other has."

"Fuck him!" Wisdom shouted. "He's not my fucking brother! He's no kin of mine! Yo, he tried to fuck my girl!"

"What makes you think I tried?" I asked, wiping the blood trickling from my mouth. I smiled. "Yo, bro, that shit was slippery wet!"

Wisdom tried to charge at me, but Uncle Lou held him back.

"Stop it! Stop it!" Aunt May screamed. "Ya'll are not going to be the death of me. I'm too old for this! I've been nothing but good to you boys," she cried. "I did my part in raising you. And I did a damn good job!You two are grown now," she looked from Wisdom back to me. "But I'm tired now," she said. "I'm tired. Now if you two want to fight and kill each other do it elsewhere. Because I am not going to tolerate it in this house!"

I wasn't trying to hear any more of this shit so I quickly stormed off to my bedroom, threw on some street clothes and grabbed my gun.

Wisdom

I had been so wrapped up in arguing with Chance that I hadn't even noticed Imani leaving the house. I drove around North Philly for twenty minutes looking for her until I finally located her at the intersection of 29th and Master Street with her suitcase in tow.

Easing the car alongside her, I shifted the gears into Park and hopped out my '90 Ford Taurus. "Imani," I yelled.

She turned to look at me briefly before she kept walking.

"Imani," I repeated.

"Go away, Wisdom!" She turned around and said. "Oh, wait. You are Wisdom, right?"

I ran up to her. "Imani, you don't even know where you're walking. It's dangerous out here."

I was completely caught of guard when she whirled around and slapped the hell out of me. And unfortunately in the same spot where Chance had punched me.

"Can we please get in the car and talk now?" I asked her.

She looked at the ground and nodded her head. Gratefully, I picked up her suitcase and headed to the car.

"I'm not going back to that house," she said once inside the car. "I am not," she repeated in a shaky tone.

"I understand," I said. "Look, you don't have to tell me what happened. You don't ever have to talk about it again. Yo, we could just forget tonight even happened."

Imani was silent as she stared out the window at a wino stumbling up the street.

"I could drive us back up to Massachusetts right now—"

"No," Imani surprisingly said.

"No?" I repeated. I had to be sure I heard her right.

She turned to face me. "We can stay. I don't want to be the reason you have to leave early. I see how excited your aunt is with you around. She misses you." she said. "So I want to stay. But I will not spend another night in that house."

"Okay," I reached over and touched her face. "We'll get a room somewhere."

Imani and I had decided to check into Sweet Dreams Hotel located on Germantown Avenue. I had to work out all the bullshit that had occurred over a mere few days. There had never been this much static between me and Chance. I couldn't leave Philly with all this shit over my head. As fucked up as Chance was he was still my brother and I couldn't leave things the way they were. Unlike him, I had a conscience.

Chance

"What happened to your face?" Keisha asked, standing behind the screen door, with her hands on her hips.

I looked past her at CJ. He was sitting on the living room floor playing with Micro Machines without a care in the world. Deep down I knew the kid was mine. Not only did he have my name, he had also inherited my eyes, my nose, my ears, and my skin tone. I didn't know why I was denying the little boy. It wasn't his fault that I was scared about the idea of being someone's father. Shit, I never had mines in the picture. Never even seen the motherfucker. And regardless of me never meeting him, I hated him. I hated him because unfortunately I was just like him. Too afraid to accept responsibility.

"Can I come in?" I asked her.

She crossed her arms, and rolled her neck. "Why? So you can hit me again?"

I looked down at the ground, unable to meet her gaze. I didn't know what the fuck was going on with me lately. As much as I hated to admit it, I did wish I could be more like Wisdom. But instead I was too busy being Chance. Why couldn't I just get my shit together? Maybe go to school. Get a degree. Get a good job. And move my baby mama and kid up out the Gracy Home Projects.

"Yo, you pushed a nigga that far," I said defensively.

Imani held her long ass fingernail up to her face. "Why can't you just be a man and apologize."

I exhaled deeply. Looked around at the dilapidated project houses Keisha called "home."

"Look, baby," I sighed. "I'm sorry about that shit earlier." I fished in my jeans and pulled out the wad of cash I'd robbed the convenient store of. "I got a little money for you and the baby."

Keisha sucked her teeth. "I don't want your fucking money, Chance. I want you to be a father to your child! I'm sick of you denying him."

A few units down, a man stepped out of his apartment to smoke a cigarette. The motherfucker thought he was slick but he wasn't. I hated nosy ass people.

"Look, baby. I promise I'm gonna get my shit together." I told her. "But you just gotta--Yo, what the fuck you looking at!?" I lashed out at the guy. He was looking at Keisha and I like we were an episode from a soap opera or some shit.

He tossed his hands in the air and slowly retreated back to his unit.

"Yo, Keish, just let me in, so we can talk. You know I don't like people in my damn business."

She rolled her eyes and considered it for a moment, before finally allowing me entrance into her home.

She threw her hands back on her hips, "So? Talk!"

"Let's talk in the room, I don't want my son hearing this," I told her.

She looked down at our son, looked back up at me, and sucked her teeth. "Alright."

I watched her ass in the white cotton robe she was wearing as she sashayed towards her tiny 9x9 bedroom. Once we were inside, I closed the door behind us.

"Okay, so—"

Before she could finish I grabbed her in my arms, crushing my lips against hers. She tried to fight the kiss at first, but eventually relaxed. She threw her arms around my neck, our tongue exploring each other's mouth. My dick pressed against the crotch of my Levis. I had to get out of these jeans. Get my dick in something warm and yet.

I couldn't move fast enough as I snatched Keisha's robe off and pushed her backwards onto her full-size bed.

She eagerly unbuttoned my jeans as I eased the gray hoodie over my head.

"Hold on," I told her, pulling the pistol from the back of jeans.

Keisha followed the gun with her eyes as I placed it on her wooden nightstand.

"What the hell is that, Chance?" she asked with a look of uneasiness.

"It's nothing," I said, as I climbed in bed, positioning my face at her waist. "Open your legs," I whispered, before burying my tongue in between her thighs.

She arched her back, ran her fingers through my short curly hair as I licked and lapped at her juices, suckled her swollen clit, and slid my tongue in and out of her slick opening.

"I want you to ride me," I told her, climbing up beside her.

"You got a condom," she asked as she straddled me.

"Come on now. What we need a condom for?" I asked.

She sucked her teeth. "So we don't end up with another one of those," she said, pointing her head in the direction of the closed door. "You can't even take care of the one you got now. You have a hard enough time not denying him."

I caressed her breasts, writhed her nipples between my fingers to keep my dick from going limp. "I'm gonna start being the father and man you want me to be," I told her. "I promise I'm gonna get a job and take care of you. I'm gonna move you up out this joint."

Keisha smiled as she eased her moist pussy over my dick. "Word?" she asked.

I gripped her hips as I told her, "Hell yeah, I promise girl."

Keisha was only eighteen but she rode me like she'd been fucking for twenty-something years. That's why I couldn't get enough of her ass. She bounced and gyrated on my dick like she had something to prove. And in a way I guess she did. She thought she could fuck me into being a good man to her and a good father to my son. Little did she know she couldn't use that "sex weapon" shit on my ass no matter how much she believed she could trap me. No matter how good the sex was I unable to be manipulated by it, and that's exactly why she threw a fit the minute I climbed out of bed and began pulling my clothes on.

"So this is what you came over here for? Again?" she cried, sitting up in bed.

I ignored her as I pulled my jeans on.

"Answer me." she yelled. "I'm sick of you coming over here, fucking me, and then leaving me here to take care of your child by myself!"

I sat on the edge of the bed with my back turned to her as I pulled on my Adidas.

"You ain't shit, Chance," she cried.

I ignored her as I stood up, dug into the back pocket of my jeans and tossed the stolen money on her nightstand.

"I told you, I don't want your fucking money!" she screamed, knocking it all on the floor.

I ignored her as I walked out of the room, past my son, past my responsibility.

"You ain't shit, Chance!" she screamed out after me.

I didn't say a word as I left the apartment. After all what   could   I   say?

Wisdom

"Imani, you asleep?" I asked, softly nudging her. The plush bedding of the queen size bed had put Imani to sleep the minute her head hit the pillow.

I pressed my dick against her lower back, hoping she'd wake up.

"What do you want, Wisdom," she whispered agitated.

Would it make me insensitive if I told her what I wanted? Even after everything that had happened tonight?

I bent down and kissed her ear.

She slowly turned around to face me, placed a soft kiss on lower lip.

"I love you," I whispered.

She kissed my chin. "I love you too."

I reached over and grabbed the condom off the nightstand. Slowly climbing on top of her, I positioned myself between her thighs after rolling the rubber down my shaft. "How much you love me?" I asked, as I guided myself inside of her.

She gasped upon my entrance, relaxed a bit. "Do you really to have to ask?" she smiled.

I leaned down, kissed her, and held her, as I filled her with soft, gentle thrusts. She ran her fingers through my short curly hair as I buried my face in her shoulder, allowing myself to plunge deeper into her wetness. I stroked her insides, using sex to substitute the things I should have said like: "Baby everything's going to be fine", or "I'm here for you."

"Wisdom," she whispered, pressing her pelvis into mine.

I kissed her deeply, passionately. She knew how I felt without me even having to say it.

***

It was 9:04 p.m. when Imani and I were leaving La Casa de Sirena, when a young Hispanic woman gave me the strangest look. Standing on the curb right outside of the Mexican restaurant, it was obvious that she was soliciting. But it wasn't her outlandish attire that made her stand out. It was the hideous scars and bruises exposed on her face, arms, and legs. I tried not to make a face at the gruesome pinkish skin abrasion on the left side of her face.

I wrapped my arm around Imani's waist as we walked away from the restaurant, and pretended I didn't notice her staring at me the entire time. However, after several seconds she quickly ran across the street, dodging a few passing cars in the process.

Instantly I felt my stomach knot up. I had a bad feeling about that woman.

Imani turned her head to see what was causing the screeching tires and beeping horns. "What was that about?" she asked.

I ignored her as I watched her run up to a Ford Explorer parked underneath a street light, right across the street from *La Casa de Sirena*. After the driver quickly rolled its window down she began eagerly pointing in my direction.

"Come on, Imani," I said, speeding up the pace. We had parked around the corner, and I couldn't get to my Taurus fast enough. I wasn't in the mood for any bullshit.

I turned to look over my shoulder, and saw the prostitute climb into the back of the truck.

"Let's go," I grabbed Imani by her elbow and began speed walking to my car.

"What's going on?" Imani asked.

The truck quickly sped off and I knew they were coming after me. But for what reason, I had no idea.

I yanked Imani along as I broke into a full on sprint towards the car.

"What's happening?" Imani screamed in fear.

The moment we reached the corner, the truck executed a sharp left turn burning rubber in the process. With trembling fingers I jammed the key into the keyhole, missing it the first two attempts. I quickly unlocked the car, jumped in and reached over to unlock the door for Imani. Three men hopped out of the truck at the exact same moment Imani climbed in.

I only caught a glimpse of the black metallic object, before it came crashing through my window. Glass shattered and spilled in my lap. Imani screamed. Everything was happening all too fast. The car keys dropped into the car seat gap. I didn't get a chance to look at my aggressor before he slammed his gun into my jaw. Imani screamed again.

The attacker reached into the car, unlocked the door and dragged me out at the exact same moment another assailant snatched Imani from the passenger seat.

"Leave her alone!" I screamed.

Suddenly the air was knocked out of me, as the attacker punched me in stomach, I keeled over in pain instantly.

"Pick his ass up!" The man said.

I struggled to look up. "Please...don't h--hurt her," I cried.

The man was tall, dark skinned, and looked to be in his mid thirties. He was wearing a black and white Addidas track suit and black Kangol hat. A toothpick was hanging out the corner of his lip, and a gold rope chain dangled loosely around his neck.

"Don't hurt her? Don't hurt her like you hurt my bitch?" he spat.

I looked down at the floor, "I don't know what you're talking about?"

"Roxie?" he barked. "Roxie get your ass out here?"

I heard the click-clacking of her knee high heels and forced myself to look up at her. Her wounds were even more gruesome up close and I wished I could slap the shit-eating grin off her ugly ass face.

"Bitch, is this the nigga or what?" he asked.

Roxie looked me over for a mere two seconds, puffing on a cigarette. Smiling, she said, "Yeah, Ghost. That's him. I'm sure of it." She nodded her head. "That's the motherfucker that robbed me and pushed me out of the fucking car!"

Ghost gave me a disgusted look as he chewed on his toothpick. "Yo, I hate a nigga that lies—"

"She's lying!" I screamed. "I've never seen her in my life!"

"It's him papi!" she yelled. "He made me suck his dick and swallow! Then he took my money and did this to me!" she screamed, pointing to the side of her face.

"She's lying!" I screamed.

Ghost pulled the toothpick from his mouth and tossed it onto the asphalt. "Hold that motherfucker still."

"Wisdom!" Imani screamed.

I writhed in the man's grip, but he was too strong to get away from. Before I saw it coming, Ghost punched me in right in the nose. The bone-crunching sound was distinctive and at first the only pain I experienced were my tear ducts stinging. When the pain finally came to, my knees gave out. I felt my entire face begin to throb. The pain was totally unbearable. Blood oozed from my nose and seeped into mouth.

"Hold him still," Ghost said as I vehemently began coughing up blood.

"Leave him alone!" Imani screamed.

Ghost grabbed me by my hair, pulled my face close to his. "Ain't so funny when the shoes on the other foot," he screamed. He reached in my pants pocket and snatched out my wallet.

"Is that what you want? Take it! Take the damn money!" I yelled. "But I didn't push anyone from a car."

After fishing through it, he pulled out two twenty dollar bills. "All you got in here is forty dollars?" he asked. "You owe me another forty. But it's cool. I'll just get the rest of the money out of her ass," he said smiling in Imani's direction, revealing a seat of shiny gold teeth.

I screamed. "Leave her alo"--

Ghost had quickly delivered a gut-wrenching punch to my lower abdomen. I instantly spit up a mouthful of blood, but that didn't stop him from hitting me in the stomach once again. The man holding me mercilessly dropped me onto the pavement.

"Yo, what you think, Bobby? You think I could get some money for this jawn?" Ghost asked, pointing at Imani.

Imani cried and writhed in the man's grip. "Wisdom, please help me!"

Ghost began cackling as he looked around at the few people who were watching all of this shit take place, too scared to do anything to help. No one wanted anything to do with another person's drama.

Suddenly Roxie walked over to Imani and pressed the lit cigarette butt into her cheek.

The sound of Imani crying and screaming brought tears to my eyes. Being her man, it was my job to protect her at all costs. But now I was unable to do just that.

"I told you we'd find your ass," Roxie said, smiling at me.

"Leave her the fuck alone," I screamed, struggling to stand up.

Suddenly the bottom of Ghost's Nike Force's connected with my forehead. The back of my head smacked the concrete harshly and I quickly found myself losing consciousness.

Ghost stood over me, pulled the gun from the back of his track pants, and aimed it down at me. "I usually kill dumb motherfuckers like you," he spat. "But I got something worse in store for your ass."

Blackness began to engulf me, but not before I heard him say, "Put her ass in the truck."

Chance

I hated hospitals. Hospitals were associated with death. And when I thought about death, I thought about my mother.

"Oh, my Lord! Oh, my Lord!" Aunt May cried, as Uncle Lou and I followed her to the trauma bay, where Wisdom was located.

The minute I saw the police I stopped in my tracks, and refrained from entering the room.

"Oh, my baby. Look at my baby, Lou," Aunt May cried, nearly going into hyperventilation.

I couldn't blame her. Just the sight of seeing my brother like that sent me on edge. His head was covered with bandages, both of his eyes were blacked and bruised, and his nose was covered with a splint.

"You said his name was Ghost?" one of the officers repeated, scribbling the name down on a minute yellow pad.

"Yeah. His name was...Ghost." Chance groaned a little. "He was tall, and...," he looked as if he were losing consciousness. "I think...he had a bald...head," he said slowly, coming to again. "They took...Imani," he whispered before dozing off again.

"We gave him something for the pain." A nurse explained. "It's best if he gets some sleep. Maybe you could come back tomorrow when he feels a little better. We might keep him for a couple of days for observation. He was assaulted pretty bad."

I turned away from my brother, unable to bear seeing him in the condition he was in. I pressed my back against the hospital's cold wall and exhaled. Of course I knew who Ghost was. You couldn't be from the streets and not know who the motherfucker was. I didn't know the nigga personally, but I had indeed heard enough of him to know he was no hoe! Unfortunately, I had no idea the bitch I pushed out the car was one of his. I looked down at my feet and sighed. My brother had suffered for some dumb shit I had done. Of course, this wasn't his first time he'd mistakingly gotten his ass kicked for the something I'd done (and it probably wouldn't be the last) but this definitely turned out to be the most serious. I couldn't let this shit slide. And now Imani was missing?

This shit was fucked up!

This shit couldn't be happening!

Without deliberation, I turned and walked out of the hospital with only one destination in mind.

Johnny finally answered the door after four minutes of me pounding on the screen. "Yo, you know what time it is?" he yelled, wiping the residue from his eyes.

"It's time to go hunting, nigga. Get dressed."

Johnny looked at me as if I'd lost my mind.

But I had lost that thing long before all of this shit had even happened.

My brother was lying in a hospital bed, and all I could think about was putting a bullet in this nigga, Ghost's head.

***

It was three in the morning, and Johnny and I were cruising around, looking for someone that would be willing to give up some information about Ghost for the right price. Considering there were only hoes and dope boys on the strip at this time of night, I knew a candidate wouldn't be hard to find.

"Hold, on. Slow down," I told Johnny. "Pull over there," I pointed to a female standing on the corner. She was bopping her head as if she had a built in radio in her head or some shit. Her blonde jumbo box braids were pulled to the top of her head. She was wearing a black, fishnet shirt, black leather shorts, and red platform Go-Go boots.

Johnny broke out laughing. "Yo, don't tell me you know that jawn?"

I smiled. "I don't know her." I told him. "But I did let her slob on my pole a few times. Pull up on her."

Johnny shook his head at me as he eased his car alongside her.

"Yo, kill that shit," I said, as I rolled my window down. "What's up, Candy, baby?"

She smiled as she quickly sashayed over to the car. The minute she recognized me she turned around and walked away.

"Come on now. Don't do me like that."

She turned back around, but stayed several feet from the car. "Uh-uh, motherfucker, you stood me up last time. I can't fuck with you no more. Shit, you still owe me money."

"It ain't even like that tonight. I just want to ask you some questions. That's all." I assured her.

She propped a hand on her hip and rolled her neck as she said, "I don't give a fuck what you want. Time is money, motherfucker, and you ain't good on your word!"

I sighed at her antics. Why was she making this shit harder than it had to be? Now if I climbed out the car and whooped her ass I was sure she would talk then. I tried to let self-control do it's job as I turned to face Johnny. "Yo, give me twenty-dollars."

He looked at me as if I'd just sprouted a third eye in the middle of my forehead. "Twenty dollars?" he repeated sarcastically.

"Yeah, twenty dollars." I repeated with more authority.

Johnny looked over at Candy then back at me. "Yo, you about to give this ugly bitch twenty dollars?" He had purposely said it loud enough for Candy to hear. She quickly flipped him off after the comment.

I looked at her and smiled. "You heard the young lady. Time is money."

Johnny sucked his teeth as he dug into the pocket of jeans. "Yo, I wouldn't spit on a dime and give it to that bitch."

After he handed me the bill, I waved it out the window. Like a fish swimming to take the bait, she sprinted towards the car. She latched onto the bill but I wouldn't let it go. "You gonna answer some questions for me?"

She brushed a long braid from her face. "Sure. What you want to know?"

I reluctantly let go of the bill and watched her greedily shove it down her bra.

"I know you know some cat named Ghost right?"

She looked me up and down, kept bopping her head, like her jam was playing in her head. "Yeah, I know him. I don't work for him. But I know him," she quickly added.

"You think you can tell me everything you know about him?"

She stopped bopping her head, and smiled, revealing a few gold caps in her mouth. "Uh, shit. What are you going to do? Make a move on the nigga?"

I put on my best "I'm-not-fucking-around face. She got the point.

"He, um, he's this old school cat that be running hoes up in North and South Philly."

"Word?"

"So what ya'll fools planning? I know ya'll plotting some shit," she smiled and ran her thick, pink tongue across a gold tooth.

"I paid your ass to answer the questions, not ask them." I told her.

"I was just saying," she began defensively. "If you were trying to run up on him, he's never alone."

"Word?" That was Johnny.

"He usually be around Center City when he's not busy babysitting his hoes."

"So what this cat look like? I never even seen the motherfucker before." Johnny said.

She smirked and went back to bopping her head. "Just look for the motherfucker that looks like the fourth member of Run DMC." she joked. "He drives a black Explorer."

I smiled. "Cool, thanks Candy."

She propped her hand on her hip. "Yo, you sure you don't want no head?"

***

Johnny and I drove around North Philly, Center City, and parts of South Philly looking for this cat. At 7 a.m. we finally called it a wrap.

"You sure you want to do this?" Johnny asked on the way back home.

I hoped this fool wasn't bitching out on me.

"My brother is laying up in the hospital. His girl is missing. All because of the shit I did." I turned to face him. "You really think I'm gonna let this shit slide?"

All Johnny had was his older brother after their parents were killed in a car crash. I figured if anybody could relate to how I was feeling now it would definitely be him.

"Aye, I'm not trippin' on you," he said. "We gets down when it comes to our fam'."

"You already know."

"Yo, so you talked to Keisha lately?"

I knew Johnny was just trying to change the subject but I really didn't want to talk about her ass now. "Man, I ain't thinking about that bitch."

Johnny sucked his teeth and shook his head. "I don't know why you be doing her fine ass like that."

I chuckled. "She might be fine, but her looks ain't worth headache."

"Word?"

I ignored Johnny as I caressed the barrel of the gun with the tip of my fingers. "I'm putting a bullet in that nigga's head before it's all said and done," I promised.

<u>Chance</u>

I was happy to see that my brother was up and functioning well this morning. He almost had me in tears seeing him the way he was last night. I half expected him to go into details about everything that happened but I was grateful that he didn't. Apart of me knew he was aware of the fact that I was somehow involved in this mess.

Aunt May cracked open a can of ginger ale for Wisdom and placed it on his breakfast tray.

"Thanks," he forced a weak smile. "But I'm not handicap, Aunt May."

"Well, if you're not handicap, then when will they be releasing you?" Uncle Lou fussed. "I hate hospitals."

Aunt May cut her eyes at him. "Hate is such a strong word."

Wisdom shuffled around in his hospital bed and stared through the room's window. "Nurse says I should be discharged sometime this afternoon."

I looked around the cold, stale room. I had nothing to say. What could I say?

"Did you get in touch with Imani's parents?" Wisdom asked, still looking out the window.

Aunt May looked down at her chubby hands. She opened them, then closed them tightly. Uncle Lou walked over to her and put an arm around her shoulder.

She sighed. "Yes. I spoke with the mother. And believe you me, it was an unpleasant conversation."

I shuffled from one foot to the other with my back against the wall. I need to smoke something.

The room remained quiet for several seconds.

Suddenly Aunt May said, "They'll be in town this evening."

I couldn't take hearing anymore of this shit.

"I need some fresh air," I mumbled, before sliding out the door. Just as I was walking out of the room, a well groomed white man was heading inside. He was wearing a navy blue suit, with a black and white pinstripe tie. On his feet were black polished loafers. His salt and pepper hair was mostly silver at the temples. He had confidence in his stride.

Naturally I stopped in my tracks and stood outside the door to eavesdrop.

"Hello, good morning. I'm sorry for intruding. My name is Detective Moretti. I'm with the 23rd Precinct. I just have a few questions for you and I'll be on my way. Is that alright?"

"Okay," Wisdom mumbled.

"First and foremost, are you able to give me a description of the assailant? Race? Age? Height? Weight? Eye col—"

Wisdom sighed in frustration. "He was black. Dark skinned. I don't know how old he was. I'm guessing mid to late thirties. His name was Ghost. Look, I talked to police last night. Why am I answering these questions again? Shouldn't you be out there looking for Imani?" Wisdom yelled.

"Whoa, slow your breaks Mr. Ainesworthe. I'm only here to help."

"Calm down, Wisdom," Aunt May urged.

"It's to my knowledge that you weren't in the best condition last night to give a clear description, so here I am now. And I promise if you work with me, I'll work with you." he explained. "So once again, I'm going to need that description so we can find this bastard."

Not before I do.

Wisdom sighed and sat up in his hospital bed. "He was black. I think he had a bald head. He was wearing a hat. He was around six foot one. Maybe taller."

"Can you remember his clothing?" Moretti asked.

"Um...not really."

"Do you remember what your girlfriend was wearing?" he asked while jotting down notes in his yellow note pad.

"She was wearing a jean jumper with a pink t-shirt underneath," Wisdom eagerly answered.

"Okay. Now that that's out of the way, I have to ask this. Do you have any idea why this person would want to harm you or your girlfriend?"

Suddenly my heart felt as if it had sank into the pit of my stomach as I awaited my brother's response.

"I, uh...I'm not sure."

Moretti looked Wisdom over as if he were trying to read him. "Okay then," he finally said. "Thank you for your cooperation." He turned to walk out of the room at the exact same moment I pressed my back against the wall, heaving a sigh of relief.

Moretti peered at me standing beside the door, looking suspicious as hell.

"Can I talk to you for a second?" he asked, stepping a few feet away from me.

"What do you need to talk to me for?"

"I just want to ask you some questions. Is that okay?" His tone was casual but his expression said: Please kid don't fuck with me.

I reluctantly walked over to him.

I stared at the tile as I nodded my head.

"Any reason why someone would do this to your brother?"

I sighed. "No reason. But you know how it is."

Moretti cut his eyes at me. "How is it?" he asked sarcastically.

"People do shit for the hell of it if they know they can get away with it." I explained.

A smirk tugged at the corner of his thin lips.

"Oh, is that right?" he asked.

"Well...yeah," I hesitated.

Something told me I was sticking my foot in my mouth.

"Do you know anything about a robbery that happened up on Quincy Avenue?" he asked. "It took place a couple of days ago."

So this is the real reason the motherfucker wanted to talk to me.

"I didn't hear anything about Abduhl's being robbed."

He licked his lips, and furrowed his brow. "Who said Abduhl's had been robbed?" he asked.

"You said—"

"I said Quincy Avenue. I didn't say the name of the store."

"There's only one store up on Quincy Avenue," I argued.

"I beg to differ but there's several depending on how far up Quincy we're talking. There's a pawn shop. A fast food restaurant. An electronic store. A video store. A novelty shop." He chuckled, using his fingers to count off the stores. "Now you tell me why out of all the places I named, Abdhul's is what came out of your mouth? How did you just assume Abduhl's had been robbed since you heard nothing about the robbery?"

My mouth was dry. I was at a loss for words. I forced myself to swallow the lump that had formed in my throat. "I think I did hear something about it," I choked out.

Moretti shook his finger in my face. "I already had a look at your juvenile criminal record before I came here. You're only nineteen and your rap sheet is deplorable, Mr.

Ainesworthe..." he paused. "I have a hunch you know exactly why someone would do this to your brother."

I looked this motherfucker up and down and twisted my face up. "Yo, man. You don't know me." My voice was calm but I was fuming inside. Who did this motherfucker think he was?

The detective exhaled deeply, ran his fingers through his salt and pepper hair, and looked around the hallway before his eyes landed back on me.

He patted me on the shoulder and said, "For now those are all the questions I have for you. But trust I'll be in touch."

"Yeah, whatever man."

I watched him disappear inside the elevator at the end of the hallway, wondering why he didn't take me in when he had more than probable cause. Something told me I'd see him again...and soon.

Wisdom

"Wisdom, baby, you have to eat something."

I ignored Aunt May as I flipped through every news channel I could find.

She sighed as she headed back towards the kitchen.

"How you feeling?" Uncle Lou asked, gently moving my feet from the sofa so he could take a seat.

I ignored him as I continued clicking buttons.

He exhaled deeply. "Wisdom, you can't keep torturing yourself like this. All you can do is put it in God's hands."

Tears welled up in my eyes as I said, "I brought her here."

"Wisdom—"

"This is my fault!" I blurted out as tears streamed down my face. "If something happens to her, Unc," I wiped away at the mucus trickling from my nose. "I don't know if I can live with myself."

"Wisdom, you couldn't have foreseen this."

"I didn't do shit when he took her, Uncle Lou. I was supposed to protect her. I was"--

Before I could stop it from happening, the waterworks came. Uncle Lou held me as I cried. I cried because there was nothing else I could do. Or was there?

I quickly broke away from Uncle Lou and stood up. "I can't just sit here and wait, Unc. I have to do something."

"Wisdom, let the police do their job," Uncle Lou said with a look of concern.

I grabbed my car keys from the side table and headed out the door.

Chance

"I put a little word out there for niggas to keep their eye on the lookout for this cat. It's only two of us and Philly's a big city. A couple more pairs of eyes will help."

I gave Johnny dap. "Good looking."

"Oh, yeah, you already know. So did you hear anything about...?"

"They mentioned her a few times on the news, but they ain't find shit. I doubt they will."

Johnny shook his head as he puffed on a blunt and stared at the row of houses across the street. Directly across from us were a group of little girls drawing on the sidewalk with chalk. "That's a damn shame," he mumbled.

"Yo, tell me about it."

Johnny passed me the blunt and I took a long drag on it. There was something different about the atmosphere. Besides the gray sky, today seemed incredibly depressing.

I took one more puff on the joint before giving it back to him. "Alright, homie, I'll catch up with you later."

We gave each other dap again before he left.

"Where was Wisdom going?" I asked Uncle Lou. He was sitting on the couch with a faraway look in his eyes.

He sighed. "He went to look for that damn girl," he whispered.

I joined him on the floral print couch. "Something told me you were gonna say that. He know he needs to let the police do their job."

Uncle Lou threw his hands in the air. "That's what I told him. But you know he's just like you. Hardheaded." He shook his head.

Suddenly Aunt May walked into the kitchen, with a tray of sandwiches. "I made everyone some turkey sandwiches," she said placing the tray on the wooden coffee table in front of us. "Eat up."

I didn't have much of an appetite these last few days but I still forced myself to pick up a sandwich and bite into it. I felt like I was eating paper as I chewed on the sandwich. Aunt May was one of the best cooks I knew, but stress had a way of making things taste less appealing. I quickly replaced the sandwich on the plate.

Aunt May took a seat on the recliner chair. "Anything?"

Uncle Lou and I said "Nope" at the same time.

She sighed. "Where's Chance?"

"Aunt May I'm right here."

She chuckled. "Wow, I haven't done that in a while. Where's Wisdom?"

I looked over at Uncle Lou, unsure if I should tell her he went searching for Imani.

"He, uh...went to get some fresh air," Uncle Lou lied.

"Oh, okay." She said. "I don't blame him."

I was glad Uncle Lou didn't tell her. Aunt May would probably faint. I knew deep down inside she cared about Wisdom more than me. She probably even loved him more. He was smarter, more respectful, and more determined. He had made her proud, and I was nothing more than a disappointment. A fuck up.

The sudden cries of thunder rumbled throughout the dark sky. It was only 6:00 p.m. but it looked as if it was going on nine.

"I hope he's okay," Aunt May said.

"He's good," I promised as I stretched out, so I could relax a little more. Before I knew it, I had quickly dozed off.

***

My eyes quickly shot open at the sound of the screen door slamming shut. My nerves had been on edge these last few days. "What was that?" I asked sitting up. Aunt May and Uncle Lou were seated in the same positions.

"Wind blowing the screen door open. It's raining pretty bad out there and Wisdom still hasn't come back."

I looked at the alarm clock above the television set. It read 9:59 p.m.

Damn.

"Maybe you and Johnny should go look for him. I'm worried about him, Chance."

As if on cue, Wisdom came walking through the front door, soaking wet.

"Wisdom, where have you been?" Aunt May asked, standing up. "You had me worried sick!"

"Mabel!" Uncle Lou shouted.

Aunt May looked over at him.

He shook his head. "Now's not the time."

"Good evening, we have new developments tonight on the body that was discovered in a North Philadelphia alley. Police were called at 7:06 p.m. to the 1600 block of North Hope Street, where the body was found and later identified as missing Harvard student Imani Buhari"-- I quickly got up and turned the television off.

Wisdom stood there with this mouth gaped open for several seconds. Me, Aunt May, and Uncle Lou held our breaths.

"Wisdom", Aunt May began.

"*Arrrrrrrrrrrrrrrrggggggggghhhhhhhhh!*"

The shit scared the hell out of me. Wisdom sunk down against the door and began crying hysterically and Aunt May covered her mouth as she silently did the same. Uncle Lou rose from the couch and headed over to Wisdom, but was surprisingly pushed away.

He quickly stood up and ran outside in the pouring rain. Uncle Lou looked over at me."Go talk to him."

I quickly ran outside where Wisdom was sitting on the front steps crying, fists balled, shaking his head. I didn't know what to say to him. I wasn't good at condoling anyone, and I couldn't promise him that I'd put a bullet in Ghost's head for Imani.

"Bro..."

In a shaky tone Wisdom asked, "Did you have anything to do with this?"

I forced myself to swallow the lump that formed in my throat, but remained silent.

Wisdom quickly jumped up. "Did you?" he screamed as he forcefully shoved me.

I stumbled backwards off the front steps and nearly twisted my ankle.

"I didn't tell the police what that motherfucker told me that night. I was too afraid to face the fact that you were somehow involved in this shit!" he shook his head vehemently, looking more like a psycho than my brother. "Just tell the truth!" Wisdom shouted. "Did you rob that woman? Did you push that woman out a fucking car?" he asked crying.

Tears formed in my eyes but I quickly blinked them away. "Bro, I'm sorry," I choked out.

"You took the one thing from me that mattered the most! Do you..." he paused. "Do you know how I fucking feel right now, Chance? Do you know how I feel," he repeated through gritted teeth.

"I...Wisdom...," I quickly wiped away at an oncoming tear. "I'm not shit." I said, hearing Keisha's voice in the back of my mind.

"This is why I stayed away for so long!" Wisdom screamed. "Because of you, Chance! You always find a way to drag me into your shit! Always," he yelled. His voice was beginning to grow hoarse. "Fucking up your life isn't enough for you, no, you have to go and fuck up mine!"

The rain was pouring down on both of us. Too bad it couldn't wash any of this bullshit away.

Suddenly Wisdom rushed me and tackled the shit out me. I landed with a thud on the wet grass and it felt as if the breath had been knocked out of me. Wisdom didn't give me time to recuperate as he wrapped his hands around my throat.

Strangely, I didn't bother fighting back. Honestly, I didn't want to. This might sound crazy but I wanted him to end this shit. End this pathetic excuse of a life.

"Kill me," I forced out as I felt my face swell up and grow hotter by the second. Tears streamed down my cheeks. Some belonged to me, the others were Wisdom's as he cried over me. He bared his teeth like a madman as he proceeded to choke me to death. "Kill me," I repeated. "You said it....yourself. I...deserve to die."

"Lou! Lou! He's gonna kill him!" Aunt May screamed from the front porch.

"Kill...me," I said, feeling myself reaching unconsciousness.

Suddenly Wisdom's grip loosened around my throat. "You're not even worth it..." he spat as he slowly stood up.

Uncle Lou limped out of the house and down the front steps as Wisdom walked to the curb in front of the house and took a seat on it.

"You alright?" Uncle Lou asked after he reached me.

I caressed my throat and coughed uncontrollably. I wasn't able to answer if I wanted to. I slowly stood up and struggled to gain my balance.

Suddenly Johnny pulled up in front of the house, beeping his horn.

It was time to go hunting.

I quickly walked in the house, into my bedroom, and grabbed the pistol from underneath my pillow.

"Where are you going, Chance?" Aunt May cried hysterically as I stormed past her. She tried to grab my arm to keep me from leaving the house but I violently pulled away from her.

"Lou, stop him! He's about to go do something stupid! I know it!" Aunt May screamed behind me.

But it was too late. I was already opening the passenger door to Johnny's car. I tried to avoid looking into the spiteful gaze of Wisdom's. He hated me and I couldn't blame him. After today, I hated myself.

Chance

"Is that the nigga?" Johnny asked as he peered through his lowered window at the black truck across the street.

We had been sitting underneath the train tracks on Kensington Avenue staring at the truck for ten minutes. What a coincidence that I found him on the same street where I pushed the hoe out of the car.

I knew we had to make a move and quick before Ghost got suspicious.

"Right about now I'll put a bullet in a nigga just for looking like Ghost."

Johnny chuckled. "Yo, I think his ass is alone." He peered through his binoculars. "Look like he's talking on the phone too. He won't even see us coming."

Normally I would've made a joke about his ass even owing a pair of binoculars but now wasn't the time.

"Let's get this shit over with," I said slowly opening up the passenger door. I pulled my hood over my head and cocked the hammer.

Johnny quickly pulled a ski mask over his head and I nearly burst into laughter at the way it looked pulled over his "gumby haircut." Then I remembered now wasn't the time for jokes. Johnny and I waited for a few cars to pass by before we sneakily crept over to Ghost's truck.

He was sitting in the driver seat with his head leaned back. I would've thought the motherfucker was taking a nap had I not saw the brick phone in his hand pressed against his ear.

I had never been this excited to do anything in my life. I wished I would have had as much determination to do something with my life as I had to kill this son of a bitch.

My heart pounded ferociously as sweat quickly formed on my forehead.

"Yeah. Okay, that's cool," I heard him say as we approached him.

He was listening to Ice Cube's "*Amerikka's Most Wanted*", unaware that his death was quickly approaching.

The gun trembled in my sweaty palm. I looked over at Johnny who was making sure there were no witnesses in sight. This was the first time either of us would do something as intense as this.

Time seemed to slow down as I quickly ran up to his lowered window and lifted the gun to his temple. It wasn't until after I pulled the trigger that time seemed to return normal.

Suddenly the same fucking prostitute I pushed out of the car began screaming. Her face was splattered with blood. I didn't even know the bitch had been in the car with her head buried in Ghost's lap.

Johnny quickly reached over and snatched the gold rope chain from Ghost's neck. My heart felt as if it would tear out of my chest as it thumped wildly. Without deliberation I fired a shot that landed right beneath her left eye. The bullet shattered the glass behind her as her head dropped into Ghost's lap.

"Hurry up!" Johnny yelled as he sprinted in the direction of his car nearly tripping in the process.

I looked down at the brick phone that was still clutched inside of Ghost's hand. Whoever was on the other end of the phone was hollering into the receiver. Just for the hell of it, I picked the phone up and placed it against my ear.

"Hello? Hello? Ghost, are you there?"

"Ghost is..." I looked over at Ghost's lifeless body, slumped over in his seat. "Incapacitated."

"Oh… I see." he said. "So, I'm guessing you just killed my footman and judging from your fast paced breathing I know you're probably in a rush, so I'll talk quick."

"Chance!" Johnny screamed.

I ignored him as I continued to listen to the mystery man on the opposite end of the phone.

"Come on tell me, how much you honestly make robbing punks? A little chump change? Yeah. That's what I thought," he said, not giving me a chance to answer.

"Meet me tomorrow at Maria's on North 5th tomorrow at seven so we can talk business. I promise you will like what I have to say."

Suddenly Johnny eased his car beside me burning rubber in the process.

"How I know you ain't gone off me for killing your boy?"

He blew air through the speaker. "Please. I'm a business man. There is no bad blood between us. As long as my operation continues I'm a happy man."

I quickly climbed into the passenger seat and said, "I'll see you tomorrow."

"Keep this phone," he ordered before disconnecting the call.

Wisdom

I didn't hear Aunt May come into the kitchen as I sat looking out the window, wishing I was somewhere other than I where I was now. This shit was not happening. No. No. No. No. No. This shit was not happening.

Aunt May didn't say a word as she began to brew a pot of coffee. She woke up every morning 6:00 a.m. so this was nothing out of the norm for her. Well, nothing except for seeing me awake in and staring out the kitchen window. I was feeling as if I was in some sort of distant place. Detached from reality. I had quickly lost my sanity. And I was afraid that it would be hard to regain. How could I go back to school and function normally? Things wouldn't be the same without Imani.

The sudden sound of porcelain hitting the kitchen table startled me, and momentarily interrupted my thoughts.

I looked over at Aunt May who had raised her coffee mug to her lips. She looked down at the mug sitting in front of me, and I hadn't even noticed she had poured me a cup. I wasn't much of a coffee drinker but I appreciated the gesture.

"I'm thinking about dropping out," I told Aunt May as I began moving the coffee mug around. I watched the cream swirl around, before lifting it to my lips.

"Don't go thinking irrationally now, Wisdom." Aunt May said. "I know these last few days haven't been easy for you, but you can't just drop out of college. It was a blessing with you even getting accepted." she said. "Wisdom, you are strong. You're able-minded, and tougher than most men you're age. You've overcome so much already. You will get through this."

I looked out the window. I expected her to say that. But she had no idea how I was feeling now. I felt as if I had been stabbed in the heart. I felt as if I was in the tight grip of inevitability. Wondering how could this happen? Why did this happen? My life felt somehow diminished. It would never be the same. My life no longer seemed so happy. So bright. So full of promise. I was completely grief-stricken that I had lost someone so important to me in life. But I was even more hurt that my brother was the cause of all of this. Right about now I didn't give a damn if they ever found Ghost or his goons. I know most people are happy to see the murderers of their loved ones behind bars, but I just didn't care either way. It wouldn't bring Imani back and it surely wouldn't offer me a sense of closure.

Things like this just don't happen do they? One minute a person is alive and well, and the next minute they are snatched away, brutally murdered, and forever gone? The realization felt surreal. Was I dreaming? This couldn't be reality. We had just been together. It wasn't that long ago I was running my fingers through her hair. Smelling her sweet, fragrant smell, kissing those thick, pouty lips. No. She couldn't be gone.

How could someone hurt her? How could someone really look her in the face, and truly hurt her? Before I knew it I was crying tears into the cup of coffee in front of me.

Aunt May reached over and stroked my hand. "It's going to be okay, baby," she whispered. "It's going to be okay."

I wanted to believe her. I really wanted to.

Chance

Maria's was a cruddy Mexican Restaurant located up on North 5th Avenue. Above the filthy restaurant were apartment units. I wondered why he picked such an estranged place to meet. Ultimately curiosity had gotten the best of me and I couldn't help but to wonder what kind of proposition he would offer me. What kind of operation was he running?

Once I reached Maria's I pushed open a big, black, wooden door. The strong smell of spices and peppers filled my nostrils as soon as I stepped inside. The restaurant was small. There were four booths to my left, and a small bar to my right with several stools aligned underneath. The restaurant was nearly empty besides three guys sitting together in the last booth of the restaurant and one man was sitting at the bar sipping on a Budweiser.

My heart skipped a beat as I looked around the small restaurant. Instead of the bartender greeting me, she instead offered a half assed smirk, and motioned with her head to go towards the back of the restaurant. My eyes wandered over to the three men sitting in a booth.

I thought about cutting out and running as fast as I could, but the man at the bar flashed the gun in his holster, instantly ruling out that idea. Besides there was no way I could outrun a bullet.

I swallowed my fear and slowly made my way over to the last booth. Suddenly the man at the bar thwarted my path. He remained silent as he motioned for me to raise my arms in the air. I reluctantly did as I was told, and allowed him to frisk me. He quickly snatched my pistol from the back of my jeans.

After he was sure that I was weapon-free he allowed me to be on my way. Once I reached the booth two of the guys stood up and walked over to the bar. I took a seat across a middle aged Hispanic man. He had a thick, black handle bar mustache. His hair was cut short beside the curly rattail that hung to the middle of his back.

"You're seven minutes late," he said. His Spanish accent was thick.

"I had to catch the bus here," I said, looking over at the men at the bar, who were intently watching me.

"I don't care. You should never be late when it comes to business."

I held my tongue even though I wanted to say a mouthful. Obviously, I didn't have the upper hand in this situation.

"My name is Santiago. What is your name?"

"Chance," I mumbled.

"Well, Chance... Pardon me, but you don't look like you could be the man I spoke with last night." He chuckled. "You're just a kid. You don't even look like you have hair on your cojones."

My jaw tensed. I didn't come here to be belittled. "Do you want to see them?" I retorted.

He stared at me blankly for several seconds and I immediately wondered if I had offended him. After all I was in no way able to defend myself against all four of these men equipped with guns.

Suddenly, he burst into laughter, smacking his hand against the table and all. The scene was extremely awkward considering he was the only one laughing.

"That was funny."

I didn't think so.

"So, are we going to talk business or what?" I asked flatly.

Suddenly, the bartender came over and placed a tray of chile con queso in front of him. "Let's get one thing straight," he said. "I run the fucking show. Don't you forget that. You take all of that little...macho man shit," he made a gesture with his hands as if he were balling up a piece of paper. "And throw it out the window. You come at me with respect. Comprende?"

I looked over at the men who were still watching me from the bar.

"Hey. Me estas escuchando? I'm talking to you. You look at me when I'm talking to you. Your dilemma is with me." He smiled. "Not them."

My eyebrows furrowed. "Dilemma?" My palms were beginning to sweat underneath the table. I knew I shouldn't have come here. "I thought you said we had no bad blood between us."

Santiago smiled. "Relax hermano. There is no bad blood between us but that doesn't mean you aren't indebted to me."

"Indebted?" I spit the word out as if it were a bad taste in my mouth. What the fuck was he talking about?

"Yeah, you know...obligated...bound"--

"I know what it means. But what are you talking about?"

"Well. As I mentioned last night I have an operation to maintain. A close-knit operation. Ghost was...how do you say...an important asset. He was one of my main distributors. Not to mention he had a substantial amount of clientele." He looked me over. "You know what kid? I like you. And I know whatever Ghost did to piss you off he must've deserved it." He giggled. "I could've killed your ass the minute you walked in the door, but instead I'm offering you the deal of a lifetime. I'm offering...no I'm giving you his job."

"What if I don't want it," I challenged.

Santiago ran his tongue across his teeth. "Two things. One, if you didn't want it, you wouldn't have showed up. And two, I'm not giving you the option to turn down my offer. I'd hate to kill you right now and throw your body behind the restaurant. I'm pretty sure you have loved ones that would hate to watch the news and see that your body was found mutilated in a dumpster behind a Mexican restaurant." he picked up his knife, looked at it, and then looked at me. "So what it's going to be?"

He'd made his point. "What do you want me to do?"

Chance

"Where's Wisdom?" I asked Aunt May.

She was preparing the dining table for dinner and didn't look up when she said, "He left." Her response was flat.

"Left?" I repeated.

"Yes. He left early to go back to school." Her voice cracked as she spoke. "What's that?" she asked, pointing to the book bag slung casually over my shoulder.

"Oh...it's...nothing." I lied before rushing to my bedroom. Once inside, I locked my door and emptied the contents of the book bag on my bed.

"Chance! Chance, wake up!" Aunt May shouted, banging on the bedroom door.

I groaned as I snatched a pillow over my head.

"Chance, someone is on the phone for you!" she hollered.

I reluctantly dragged myself out of bed. Before I opened the door, I made sure to push the book bag under my bed.

"Who is it?" I asked.

Aunt May ignored me as she sauntered away. She was still pissed off at me. I padded barefoot to the living room and hesitantly picked the receiver up. Placing it against my ear, I cleared my throat and said, "Yeah. Hello?"

"Chance Ainesworthe, this is Detective Moretti. I was hoping you could come down to the station so I could ask you some questions."

My heart skipped a beat. Damn. I knew Wisdom and I had fell out but was he that pissed at me to resort to snitching?

I sucked my teeth and blew into the phone. "When? What time?"

"Well, I was hoping as soon as possible."

"Am I in trouble?" I asked. "I'm not gonna come down there and get the cuffs slapped on me as soon as I walk in the station, am I?"

Detective Moretti paused. "Hopefully not."

I thought about it. "Yo, I don't like the sound of that."

"Listen, I just need you to come down to the station to answer a few questions. If you cooperate you should have nothing to worry about." He explained. "Now are you going to come down to the station or am I going to have to come and get you? And in that case I might just have to slap the cuffs on you."

"Word?" I sucked my teeth. "Damn, I'll come down." I disconnected the call before he could say anything else. What the hell did we have to talk about?

After showering and eating a bowl of Apple Jacks, I caught the bus down to the 23rd Precinct. I couldn't count on both hands how many times I had unwillingly stepped through these doors.

"Yo, where can I find Detective Moretti's office?" I asked a passing black cop.

He looked me up and down with disdain written all over his face. I guessed having a badge changed his entire outlook on being a brother.

"Follow me," he said flatly.

He led me down a long, narrow hallway to the last door on my right. The name plate outside of the door read: Gino Moretti. His door was open.

I slowly made my way inside. Although I had been to this police department on countless occasions, this was my first time stepping foot inside a detective's office.

In front of a single window was a messy dark brown wooden desk. Files were stacked on top of each other beside a telephone and stationary. The office was dark and the only illumination in the room was the meager amount of light slipping through the tight blinds.

"Mr. Ainesworthe," he greeted, looking up from his paperwork. "Thank you for coming."

"Did I have much of a choice?" I said sarcastically.

"Please come in. Would you like a cup of coffee?"

I took a seat in the chair opposite of his desk. "Naw, I'm straight. So what did you wanna talk to me about?"

Moretti removed his reading glasses and ran a hand over his weary face.

"The dropped shell we found at the convenient store matches the same dropped shell we found at a crime scene two days ago. Do you know anything about this Mr. Ainesworthe?"

I exhaled deeply. Tried to play it cool. "Man, I don't know what you're talking about?"

Moretti looked me over. Scrutinized me. It immediately reminded me of Wisdom.

"So you haven't heard anything about a shooting that took place on Kensington Avenue? The victim was"...he began shuffling through a stack of papers. "Clifford Jackson. Also known in the streets as Ghost."

I relaxed in my seat and tried to look convincing. "I don't know nothing about that."

Moretti's penetrating stare couldn't intimidate me enough to tell on myself this time.

"It's funny..." he began. "He matched the exact description that was given to me by your brother."

"Well, why wasn't he arrested?" I was now growing more agitated by the minute. "Why were ya'll letting him roam the streets? An innocent girl was killed."

"I'm sorry about your friend but we issued a warrant for his arrest. Believe me. We were doing our job." He sighed. "But I guess whoever put the gun to his head took matters into their own hands."

"Yo, why the fuck are you telling me this?" I snapped. "Am I a fucking suspect or something?"

"Should you be?"

"You tell me! You the one who called me into this motherfucker!"

Silence overtook the room. The detective stared at me as I stared at the floor.

"You know what, Chance?" he said. "Besides this tough guy persona you put on...I know there's a potentially good guy underneath it all."

I rolled my eyes and blew out air at his statement.

"I know you're really a smart kid."

"Smart?" I snorted. "Shit, all I know is the streets."

Detective Moretti stared strangely at me. He then leaned back in his seat. "You know, Chance...It's never too late."

I sucked my teeth and blew out air. Truthfully I wasn't trying to hear this shit. "If I'm not a suspect and I'm not under arrest I guess that means I'm free to go. Right?"

Moretti sighed in frustration and replaced his reading glasses on his face. "Sure. You're free to go," he said with a wave of his hand.

Chance

I didn't feel like going home. I had too much on my mind and Detective Moretti had me sweating. He said I wasn't a suspect but I didn't trust his word. So much shit was happening in so little time. Imani had been killed. And I had taken a man's life. I needed to vent. Smoke.

Thirty minutes later I found myself knocking on Johnny's screen door. Unfortunately no one answered. I was disappointed as hell because Johnny usually always had something to smoke.

Ten minutes later I was catching the bus to the Gracy Home Projects. It had been a few days since my last encounter with Keisha, but I knew she couldn't stay mad at a brother forever.

For five minutes I pounded on her screen door before she finally swung the front door open. If it was anybody else she probably would've given them lip for banging on her door. Yet, when she saw me, her mouth dropped open and she began tightening the robe around her waist.

I smiled at her modesty. "Whuddup, Keish. Yo, let me in.

She began looking around nervously and something was different in her vibe.

"What's the deal?"

She looked down at her bare feet.

"What, you got a nigga in there or something?"

"Baby—"

"Yo, you better tell the nigga to roll out 'cause daddy's home."

Suddenly, me and Keisha's gaze diverted to the man approaching her in the doorway. His pants were unbuttoned and he was shirtless.

"Ch—Chance? Man, what are you doing here?" Johnny stuttered, quickly zipping his pants.

"Naw, homie. What the fuck you doing here? Ain't enough bitches in Philly to go around?"

"Come on now, it ain't like that," he said.

"Then what is like? Because to me, it looks like you're fucking my bitch."

"Baby..." Keisha whimpered looking up at me.

I looked at her in disgust. "Hoe, you ain't shit!"

It took everything in my power not to slap the hell out of her. Instead I slammed the screen door and quickly stormed off. I was pissed. No. Being pissed was an understatement. I felt betrayed by both of them. Johnny more so because he was like a brother to me. He was closer to me than my own brother. I was mad at Keisha, because as much as I fronted I truly did have feelings for the girl, whether she knew it or not. I just had a fucked up way of showing it. I was beyond pissed. Talk about friends. Whodini had warned me about cats like Johnny but I never thought he'd betray me. After all, we'd been friends since middle school.

Just as I was rounding the corner, Johnny ran up beside me. Just the mere sight of him set me off.

"Man, I thought we were boys."

"My bad, man." He was panting and trying to regain his breath. "We are boys"--

"Man, all the shit we been through together...You were like my fucking brother."

"Chance—"

"Fuck you man."

"Chance, just the other day you was dogging the bitch and saying her kid wasn't yours. You whipped her ass in front of the whole neighborhood. You can't blame me for thinking you ain't give a fuck about her!"

I looked at Johnny in disgust. "Nigga, it's the fucking principle."

"Yo, I'm sorry, bro. My bad for just saying that shit." he said. "You right. It's the principle. Ain't no woman ever came between us. I'm sorry man."

"Yeah, me too." I said before firing a single shot in stomach.

Johnny took a step back as his eyes widened in disbelief. He slowly looked down at his wound. Sadly, he didn't even see the shit coming. His eyes pooled with tears as he looked up at me in shock. His lips parted like he wanted to say something but instead blood expelled from his mouth. Suddenly, he fell forward but I quickly sidestepped him and watched his body hit the wet pavement.

Watching him choke on his own blood, I stood over him and aimed the gun down at his head. However the sight of tears sliding down his face stopped me from pulling the trigger. Suddenly something wet rolled down my cheek and it took me a moment to realize I was crying. I lowered my weapon at the same time Johnny took his last breath.

Before I could gather my thoughts I quickly took off running. I ran as fast as I could wishing I could run away from my problems. Away from the bullshit. Away from my life. Taking refuge inside a nearby alley I expelled my breakfast on the wet pavement. I dropped to my knees and stared into a puddle of rain in front of me.

The sight of my own reflection made me sick. I saw Wisdom's face staring back at me. Taunting me. Why can't you be more like me?

I slammed my fist into the puddle and turned my head away. I took a seat on the wet ground and began crying hysterically. I had fucked up. Bad.

"Chance, what did you do? What did you do?" I cried before placing the barrel of the gun against my temple. Tiny raindrops pelted against my skin as I contemplated suicide. I kept hearing Keisha's voice in the back of my mind: You ain't shit. My hand trembled as my index finger rested on the trigger. I shook my head and cried.

Suddenly, the sound of sirens brought me back to reality as several police cars whizzed by. Once they were out of sight, I dragged what little dignity I had left home.

"Are you okay?" Uncle Lou asked after I walked into the house.

"I'm fine," I answered flatly before quickly slipping into my bedroom.

I pulled the pistol from the back of my jeans and stuffed it under my pillow. Thunder and lightning tore through the night sky and before I could stop it I began crying.

<u>Wisdom</u>

I slowly made my way up the brick walkway that lead to North End Cemetery in Potomac, Maryland. The drive up here was torturous, considering the reason why I was coming to Maryland. Not to see her beautiful face. Not to touch her soft skin. I couldn't take attending her funeral service, so instead I decided to pay my respect by attending her burial. At the top of the hill was a group of thirty or so people standing around a sienna bronze casket that had not yet been lowered into the ground.

As I approached the mass of people, I could hear the sweet melodic voice of an elderly woman singing "Amazing Grace". My heart skipped a beat as I slowly made my way towards the burial site. As I joined the congregation a few heads turned in my direction, perhaps wondering who I was.

Imani's mother, Abigail was standing beside her husband. Her pale face was covered beneath the lace veil of her funeral hat. Her natural dark red hair was pulled into a tight bun. Even while grieving she was still beautiful. Just like her daughter.

Abigail turned her head slightly in my direction. She tried her best to smile, even though the attempt was futile. I nodded my head in her direction, hoping she understood and accepted my sentiments.

Suddenly, Imani's father whipped his head in my direction. "How dare you!" he screamed.

The woman quickly ceased her singing and everyone's attention was now focused on me.

"How dare you show your face at my daughter's funeral?" he yelled.

"Femi!" his wife screamed.

He quickly shoved her away from him, and approached me with fury in his eyes. Before I could react, his fist came crashing into my mouth.

I dropped to the ground instantly. A few people screamed.

Abigail quickly ran to my side. "Are you okay?" she asked.

"You've got some nerve coming here. If it wasn't for you, I wouldn't be burying my only child. My daughter!" he screamed as tears rolled down his cheeks.

"Femi, stop it!" his wife screamed, as she proceeded to helping me off the ground.

"Everyone needs to hear this!" Femi spoke up. "My daughter was drugged. Raped. And strangled to death!" he pointed to me. "And it is this man's fault." His voice cracked as he spoke. Tears streamed down his cheek. I knew he was only speaking out of pain. It felt better to have someone to blame. And unfortunately that someone was me.

People began to gasp. A few covered their mouths, while other's shook their heads at the mere presence of me.

"Femi!"

"You are not welcome here!" he screamed at me.

"Femi, I invited him," his wife admitted.

Femi gasped and looked at his wife in disgust. "You? You invited this...this..."

"Yes. I invited him." she repeated sternly.

Femi cut his eyes at me, ready to pounce on me at any given moment.

"Don't worry, Mr. Buhari. I'm leaving." I said, wiping the blood away from my busted lip. My broken nose was now throbbing like crazy, but nothing felt worse than the humiliation I was feeling.

"Good. Let us mourn in peace."

Chance

Three Weeks Later

I stood on a dilapidated corner in front a spray painted building waiting to meet up with one of my best customers. It was over ninety degrees outside, and they were supposed to have been here an hour ago. As I stood on the corner, sweating profusely, I quickly came to the realization that drug dealing was hard work. I worked all day, and went to clubs at night only to build my clientele. Sleep was a privilege, considering I had a 24 hour/ 7 days a week job. When I first agreed to start hustling for Santiago (in Ghost's place) I thought this would be easy money. Movies always depicted drug dealers' lives as glamorous and stress free. I had no idea the real thing was the exact opposite. This shit wasn't a joke. It was the real deal.

I had my work cut out for me with this job. I spent a week learning the Metric System and the weight of a gram of coke by feel. I had the shit down-pact. Rival competitors were the only challenge I faced.

"Wassup, Chance," Felicia greeted, approaching me on the corner.

"What the fuck took you so long?"

She sniffled and wiped her nose. "I couldn't get a ride. I had to walk to this motherfucker."

Pressed. "Well, I been standing out in this damn heat wave for a fucking hour. You know the price just went up, right?"

She threw her arms in the air. "What? I had to sell my food stamps to get this little change." She sucked her teeth. "Yo, Ghost would've never upped the price on me."

"Well, bitch, I ain't Ghost."

She gave me a spiteful glare and propped her hands on her hips. "Well, how much I owe you?"

Felicia had the potential to be a pretty female. I bet before crack and cocaine conquered her lifestyle she was once an attractive woman. Her hair was in short coil twists and besides her being a drug addict she actually had pretty decent skin. She was tall and slender, and even though her clothes were two sizes two big for her, I could still see the hidden curves of her body underneath.

"Forty."

"Forty?" Felicia sarcastically repeated. "Ghost usually gives me a gram for twenty bucks."

"Like I said, I ain't Ghost. Maybe next time you'll be on time."

"But all I have on me is twenty," she cried. "Come on."

"I guess you're gonna have to get that fix somewhere else."

"Chance, please," she whimpered. "Come on now." She was now hopping from one foot to the other, looking like the fiend she was. "How about we go behind the building and I suck your dick? I heard how you like a good blow job. I'll give you one of the best you ever had," she rattled on.

Although her offer was tempting, I decided to decline. It was too damn hot, and I didn't want to be standing outside any longer than I needed to be.

Naw, I'm straight. Maybe next time." I told her. "You owe me, Felicia."

She smiled, "Thanks baby."

After exchanging our offers, I began walking home. A cold shower was all I needed at a time like this. However, as I was walking up N.19th street, I noticed a tan Crown Victoria slowly pulling alongside me.

I started to ignore the car, but the driver shouted out his passenger window, "Let me give you a ride."

I stopped in my tracks and slowly approached the car. At the sudden sight of Detective Moretti I sucked my teeth and sighed. "You following me or some shit?"

"Not at all. I was actually on my way home," he said. "So do you want that ride or not? It's pretty hot outside."

Hot was an understatement. I wiped away the beads of sweat that had quickly formed on my forehead. "Yeah, I guess."

"What were you up to?" Moretti asked as I climbed into the car.

"Minding my business," I retorted.

He chuckled at my response. Shaking his head, he said, "You would give someone a run for their money. Put your seat belt on, kid."

I looked at him, rolled my eyes, yet did as I was told.

For five minutes we drove in silence, until we reached a red light.

"You know, word in the department is you've been pushing weight for Santiago."

I sucked my teeth and exhaled. I knew it was something. "Man, I'm not about to go there with you."

"I'm just giving you a head's up." Moretti explained. "We've been working hard to bring that son-of-a-bitch's empire down. And believe me, he's going down...and hard...I'd just hate to see you fall with him." Moretti threatened. Listen, kid...No matter how tough you think you are, prison is not the place for you, son."

"Man, let me out! I'm not trying to hear this shit!" I yelled.

"I'm just forewarning you—"

"Let me out!" I screamed.

Moretti quickly brought his car a screeching halt. Cars honked their horns behind him, but I paid no mind as I quickly unlocked the door and climbed out of the car.

Chance

I was out of breath by the time I reached my front door. I could hear the sound of the old, loud vacuum cleaner whining throughout the house. Aunt May was cleaning. As I made my way towards my bedroom, the sounds of the vacuum grew louder. My worst fear had come to reality as I watched Aunt May unzip my book bag and peer inside.

"Aunt May! No!" I yelled.

The book bag slipped from her hands and landed with a soft thud against the plush carpet. She placed a hand over chest and the other over her mouth. Tears pooled in her eyes as she stared at me in disappointment. However, her soft expression quickly turned into anger as she stamped her foot down on the vacuum's foot switch.

"You brought this mess in my home?" She asked through gritted teeth.

"A—um...Aunt May, I—"

Aunt May stomped over towards me and slapped the shit out of me. "Get out!" she screamed.

"Aunt May—"

"Get out of my house!"

I sighed as I walked around her and snatched the book bag off the ground.

"Yeah, take your mess with you," she said.

As I turned to walk out of my bedroom, Uncle Lou was standing in the doorway shaking his head at me. "You only get one life, Chance," he said.

I looked down at the ground as I briskly walked past them. At the sound of Aunt May crying hysterically, my heart dropped to the pit of my stomach. I slung the book bag over my shoulder, and headed to the only destination I could think of.

<u>Wisdom</u>

"Aunt May, what's wrong?"

She was crying and rambling into the phone so dramatically that I hadn't heard a word she had said.

"I just found drugs in Chance's room. I don't know if he's doing them. I don't know if he's selling them. But I kicked him out, Wisdom. I kicked him out," she cried and sniffled into the phone. "I don't know if what I did was right. I don't know if what I did was wrong. I don't want that mess in my house, but I also feel like I'm throwing him out to the wolves." she said. "Oh, Wisdom, where did I go wrong with Chance? Where? I gave him the same life as you. I treated the two of you equally. I spent as much time and commitment with you as I did with him, why is he..." her voice trailed off. "Why is he doing this to himself? Why is he throwing his life away? I pray every night that God blesses Chance to get his life together, Wisdom. I pray every single night! But it's like the more I pray the worst he gets. I know your mother is probably rolling over in her grave." she cried. "I already lost my only sister to violence. I can't lose him too, Wisdom. I just...I can't. What should I do? He's your brother, Wisdom. Tell me. What should I do? I love my nephew. And I don't want to give up on him."

I knew Aunt May wasn't going to like what I had to say next, but it was truly how I felt. "I gave up on Chance a long time ago."

Aunt May was silent as she held on to my words. For a minute I thought she might have disconnected the call until I heard her whisper, "Promise me something, Wisdom."

"What's that?" I asked.

"Promise me, you'll at least pray for him."

Wisdom

After opening the door for me, Keisha pulled me into a warm embrace. "Did you hear?" she asked. "Someone killed Johnny."

"I heard," I said, quickly pulling away. Just the sound of her saying his name set me off. "So, um...how long?"

"How long what?" she asked.

I looked at her in disgust. I hated when she played stupid. "How long were you fucking my best friend?"" I yelled.

She propped her hand on her hip. "You need to be asking 'How long was your best friend putting food in my refrigerator and buying pampers for your son'?"

My stomach churned at that realization.

"Three months," she whispered after a moment of silence.

I slowly walked over to her and pulled her into my arms. "It doesn't matter because I'm here to take care of you. I'm not going anywhere," I promised before kissing her on the forehead.

Chance

Slinging my book bag over my shoulder, I headed out the door for my daily grind.

"Chance, don't forget to pick up some baby formula!" Keisha yelled from the bedroom.

I sucked my teeth and sighed. "What kind?"

"Good start!" she hollered back.

I closed the screen door behind me and noticed Keisha's nosy ass neighbor was standing outside puffing on a cigarette, however, at the sight of me, he quickly retreated to his apartment.

"Crazy ass motherfucker," I said, shaking my head. Readjusting the book bag on my shoulder, I rounded the corner--

Suddenly something hard and heavy connected with my jaw causing me to stumble and eventually lose my footing. I looked up at one of Santiago's goons standing over me with clenched fists.

I rubbed my jaw in pain. "Yo, what the fuck?"

"Get up!" he spat, quickly snatching me off the ground. He forcefully dragged me across the street towards a white Lincoln Town Car stretch limousine.

"Man, get the fuck off me!" I yelled, writhing in his strong grip.

He effortlessly tossed me into the back seat of the limo and slammed the door in my face.

"Relax," Santiago urged in a soothing voice. He was sitting opposite of me, puffing on a Cuban cigar. Two of his bulky security guards were sitting on either side of him. A beautiful Spanish woman was sitting to the left of me. When I looked in her direction she exhaled her cigar smoke in my face.

Everyone remained silent as their gazes were fixated upon me. I tried to act as if I were at ease as I took in the impressive decor. Indirect lighting aligned the inside of the limousine. There was a minibar and entertainment center to my right. The limo oozed "Look at me and fear me!"

"What's going on, Santiago?" I asked after several seconds of silence. Truthfully I was nervous as hell, but I tried to play it cool.

"That's what I want to know," he said with a serious expression.

"What do you mean?"

He took a long drag on his cigar, before slowly blowing smoke through his nostrils.

"Yo, we good. Right? I mean, I been sizing up competitors, setting up deals, and upping purchases. I been busting my ass night and day. I been doing everything you wanted me to, right? Right?" My nervousness had quickly surfaced.

"Chance, a little birdie came to me and told me..." He took another drag on his cigar. "You've been...how do you say...interacting with the police"--

"What?" I was now sweating bullets.

"Is it true?"

"Santiago, I swear on my dead mama, I'm not fucking with the police. A detective tried to get some shit out of me and"--

"What did you say?"

"I swear, I didn't say shit! He made a couple of threats but it was a bunch of nothing. Santiago, you gotta believe me, man."

The woman beside me began trailing an artificial fingernail alongside my inner thigh but I quickly removed her hand.

"I believe you," he finally said.

I finally exhaled the breath I'd seemingly been holding forever.

"But", he quickly added, pointing his cigar in my direction. "If I find out otherwise...as sure as you put a bullet in Ghost's head. I'll put two in yours. Comprehende?"

I swallowed the lump that formed in my throat as I nodded.

"You're free to go," he said.

I quickly climbed out the limo, but not before Santiago said, "And I won't stop at killing you, Chance. I'll kill your family." He looked me dead in the eye. "You got that?"

I looked at the ground and nodded.

"So don't let me down kid."

I watched the limousine pull off. "Damn. What did I get myself into?"

Wisdom

"I'm sorry about your girlfriend, dude. I really am. But you gotta stop moping around here. You haven't been going to class. You've gotta move on, bro."

I rolled over in my twin sized bed and looked at my roommate, Ivan.

"Imani wouldn't want to see you suffering like this." he said. "Dude you haven't been eating. You gotta get out of bed and get on with your life."

I hate hearing it, but indeed Ivan was right. As much as I wanted to stay hidden underneath a cloak of my own grief, life did go on.

I slowly slid the sheet off me and sat up in bed.

"Here, I brought you something. It's not much. But you know how they are about bringing food up here."

I accepted the orange and bag of Fritos he handed me. "Thanks man."

"No prob."

I stood up and headed over to my desk, in what seemed like ages. I took a seat in the chair and opened up my copy of The Philosophy of Art.

Chance

Club X'Kape was a popular urban night club located in Center City. It was also a place I frequented, whether it be to network or to build potential clientele.

As I was shuffling through the crowd of hyperactive dancers, I bumped shoulders with a guy while heading towards the bar. Had it not been for him turning around shoving me, I might have let the harmless bump slide.

"Yo, you tryna go there!" I yelled shoving him back.

He was at least four inches taller than me. His tall flat top reminded me of Kid from House Party. He was wearing a bright yellow tank top, black cut up denim jeans, and black combat boots. If a fight was to break out between the two of us, there wasn't a doubt in my mind that he'd kick my ass, but luckily I was strapped in order to avoid such an incident.

Before I could pull my gun out on him, one of the security guards approached us and snatched Flat Top out of my face. "Aye man. I don't want to have to put you out. But you know we have a strict no fighting policy."

Flat Top snatched his arm away from the security guard. "Naw. I'm good," he smiled. "I'm good."

"You good?" the security guard repeated.

"I'm good," he assured him. He gave me one more spiteful glare before walking off.

"Aye, thanks man."

"Yo, you got me?" the security guard asked me.

We gave each other dap. "Yeah man. You already know I look out for mines." He was one of my regulars. I hooked him up and in return he watched my back. It was a fair exchange, considering how cutthroat some fellas could be when another brother was just trying to make money.

I finally made my way to the bar and took a seat on a bar stool. The bartender hastily made her way over to me. Even with the dim lighting I could see she was fine as hell.

"What can I get you?"

I smiled and ran my tongue along my lower lip. "A shot of Hennessy. And why don't you help yourself to one...on me." I flashed a crisp hundred dollar bill in hopes of impressing her.

She didn't fall for my game as she said, "Are you twenty-one? You look a little young."

I chuckled. "You don't need to know my age, baby. Because this young nigga can teach you some...uh...things."

She made a face at my comment. "Oh, sweetie." she shook her head. "You're so barking up the wrong tree."

I drew back at her comment. "Word? It's like that?"

She smiled, revealing a set of cute dimples. "Yeah, it's like that."

"Well, shit...um...we like the same thing...that's one thing we got in common. Why don't you slide me your number so I can show you what you missing out on though."

She burst into laughter at my futile attempt. Can't blame a brother for trying.

"I'll be back with that shot," she said.

I sucked my teeth, and turned my head...only to see two sexy ass women eyeballing me from the end of the bar. Shit, why was I wasting my time on this lesbian broad when I had two admirers?

I watched in wantonness as a brown skinned female, pulled a cherry from her Martini glass, and traced the wet fruit around her full lips. Her light skinned friend waved at me and smiled.

"Get those two another round of whatever they're having," I said to the bartender. After paying my fare, I made my way over to the beautiful women. "Hello, ladies."

"Hello," they said in unison.

The brown skinned honey was wearing a hot pink Spandex dress, while the light skinned one wore a tight fitting Cheetah print dress.

The brown skinned female, pulled me close to her and whispered, "What did Santa bring me for Christmas?"

I smiled at her frankness. "It's a little early for Christmas. But don't worry I got your present...right here." I said pointing to the bulge in my jeans.

She giggled as she mistook my comment to mean my dick, when in all actuality I was pointing to my wallet.

"I'm Amber," the brown honey said.

"I'm Chante," her light skinned counterpart introduced herself.

I took turns placing a kiss on both their soft, delicate hands.

"Nice to meet you Amber...Chante...Follow me."

They grabbed their drinks and followed suite. We made ourselves comfortable in a empty booth, where I extracted my wallet. Inside were several glass tubes of cocaine, containing a gram in each one.

Chance

I threw back another shot of Hennessy and watched in shock as these two bold females sniffed a line of cocaine through a tightly rolled ten dollar bill.

Amber wiped her nose and giggled."You just gonna watch or are you gonna join the fun?"

Chante winked at me, before she began shuffling around in her seat. Before I knew it she had slipped her bare feet between my legs and nestled her toes in my crotch. "Yeah. Live a little," she said.

I smiled and shook my head at them. "Live a little, huh?"

"Yeah. Live a little," Amber repeated.

Without deliberation, I slipped another tube out of my wallet and dumped the contents on the booth's table. Technotronic's "*Pump up the Jam*" was blaring through the speakers and everyone was getting down on the dance floor, while the club's colorful flashing lights reflecting off their bodies.

Flat Top was sitting at the bar with his homeboy shaking his head at me, most likely hating. I ignored his jealousy as I leaned down and proceeded to on sniffing the line of coke. Although I had been doing this gig for nearly a month, I had never sniffed this shit up my nose. And not because of that bullshit ass motto "Never get high on your own supply". It just wasn't my thing.

After I quickly snorted the line, my nose began to burn and I became teary eyed. I sniffled and began wiping away any residue that might be on the tip of my nose. A few seconds later, there was an awkward tingling sensation that started from my fingertips and shot throughout my body before settling in my toes. For a minute I thought I was having a stroke. But then again I was only nineteen. Young people didn't get strokes. Did they?

"Can teenagers have strokes?" I asked the two women as I pocketed my wallet.

They looked at each other and burst into laughter. "No." They said in unison. "At least I don't think so," Amber added.

Suddenly, my heart beat hastened and I began to feel clammy. What the fuck was happening to me?

"Could you get me a glass of water?" I asked Chante.

"Sure. Be right back."

"So, what are you doing after this?" Amber eagerly asked.

"Going home."

"Going home?" she repeated.

"Yeah. I do have a home." I joked.

"Maybe I can get an...invite?" she smiled, before winking.

Before I could respond Chante had returned with an ice filled glass of water. After consuming that refreshment, I told them, "I think I'm going to head home, now."

"Home?" Amber repeated sarcastically. I wished she would stop doing that shit.

"Why are you leaving?" Chante asked.

"I'm...uh...tired."

"How are you getting home?" Chante asked, as if she was genuinely concerned.

I had planned on calling Keisha to come and get me but I doubted she'd feel like getting up at this time of night when she had work in the morning. "I might call a cab or something."

"Nonsense, I can take you home." Chante offered.

"Oh, I can take him," Amber spoke up. She was obviously the most aggressive of the two. "And don't you need to get those wheel bearings replaced?" She asked. "You don't need to do any unnecessary driving."

Damn. She straight played her girl.

"Well...uh...okay," she said, cheeks flushing.

"Let me just run to the little girl's room, and we can go."

I was beginning to feel nauseated. This was indeed not a good first trip for me.

After Amber returned from the restroom and her homegirl, Chante secretly slipped me her number, we made our way to the parking lot.

"Damn, this you?" I asked Amber, obviously impressed by her glossy black 1990 Mercedes Benz. I was glad I had taken her up on her offer, instead of choosing to ride in the broken down hoopty. Shit, I just might toss her girl's number out...well...then again, she was easy on the eyes.

"Yes. This is my baby," she smiled proudly.

Chance

"Is this where you live?" Amber asked with distaste as she stared at the Gracy Home Housing Projects.

"For now," I told her. "But I been saving up. I'ma get something nice. Real soon."

"Word?" she smiled.

"For sure."

She licked her lips. "So you gonna invite me up?" she asked.

I laughed. "Two seconds ago you were looking scared. Now you want an invite?"

She smiled. "I sure do."

I shook my head. "Naw...I...I can't."

She stuck her lip out. "Why not?"

"My baby mama's up there."

She began pouting and fussing.

"Maybe next time," I told her. "You got my number."

She smiled. "Okay. Well...can I have a kiss for the road?"

"A kiss for the road? Shit, you can get a kiss for the road. Some dick for the road—"

"Uh-uh," she laughed. "You ain't gone get no stains in my new ride."

"I'm just fucking with you," I lied. "Come here."

I was surprised by how aggressive she was. I had definitely met my match. Her tongue wrestled with mine as we each tried to overpower one another's dominance. She sucked on my tongue and caressed my dick through my jeans with one hand. I was in pure euphoria and I didn't know if it was because of her or the cocaine. She had me ready to strip her clothes off and bend her over the hood of her ride. Fuck this being her new car. She had taken me there.

"Don't forget to call me," I told her after our sensational kiss ended.

"I promise," she smiled.

I reluctantly climbed out of her ride and headed towards the grimy housing developments I called home.

"Damn that girl," I said to myself, looking down at my erection.

As I opened Keisha's screen door, I heard the distinctive sound of someone's footsteps approaching me from behind. Just as I was turning my head to see what was going on, something cold and hard pressed against the back of my head.

"Don't fucking turn around," the guy said as he harshly shoved my face into the door. "Where is it?"

"Where is what?" I asked.

He pushed the gun harder against my head. "Motherfucker, don't play dumb. In case you haven't realized it by now, your ass is being robbed. Now where's that fucking wallet?"

I assumed the armed man had to have been Flat Top or some hating ass nigga that had been watching me closely at the club.

"Man, damn. Hold on. Let me get it. It's in my pocket. Fuck. A nigga can't have shit," I complained.

"I suggest you shut the fuck up. Yah'mean?"

I went to fetch the wallet, but both of my pockets were empty. "It's...damn...It was just in my pocket-- Fuck!" I yelled. "That bitch robbed me! Scheming ass hoe!"

Suddenly the front door swung open and Keisha stood in the doorway.

"Chance?" At the sight of the gunman, she began to scream.

"Bitch, shut the fuck up!" he yelled.

Suddenly CJ began hollering and screaming from the bedroom.

"Where is the fucking stash?" he yelled. "I better leave this motherfucker with something or you gone get a bullet, she gone get a bullet, and that fucking baby gone get a bullet!"

Keisha quickly ran off to retrieve the book bag, where I stashed the drugs and all the money I had earned over the little time I had been hustling. Damn, my stupid ass should have gotten a bank account like everyone else.

"This is fucked up," I said, with my arms in the air.

Keisha tossed the book bag at his feet.

He bent down and unzipped the book bag. "Damn. Thanks," he said, before hitting me in the back of the head with the gun.

I fell to the kitchen floor immediately. Things began to go fuzzy as I watched a roach scurry past me and disappear underneath the refrigerator.

"Chance!" Keisha screamed, as she knelt down beside me. "Chance get up!" she screamed.

Chance

Two Keisha's fused into one fussy Keisha. She was sitting on the dirty kitchen floor with my head in her lap as held a cold wash cloth against my forehead.

I touched the back of my head and winced in pain. "Damn. How long was I out?"

Keisha sniffled, and wiped a tear away. "About ten minutes."

I looked over at the front door.

"He left right after he hit you," Keisha said.

"Damn!" I yelled. "He took everything, Keisha!"

A tear dropped from her eye and landed on my cheek. "I don't know if I can do this with you, Chance." she said, with a hoarse voice. "I mean, at first I didn't mind. You were finally taking care of me and the baby...but...Chance, that man threatened to put a bullet in my...our son!"

I sat up and grabbed the back of my head. A large knot had quickly formed. "He's the last motherfucker I got to worry about." I told her. "Now I gotta explain to Santiago why I'm missing over three thousand dollars in cocaine."

Chance

Santiago provided the cocaine and I sold the product at a higher cost than what it was worth. I kept fifty percent of all earnings. It was a unique business operation Santiago orchestrated, but I raked in over three thousand dollars a week so I didn't have a problem with that. Well...I didn't have a problem up until now.

"Do you know what time it is?" Santiago hissed into the phone.

I looked over at the digital alarm clock on Keisha's night table. It was 5:23 a.m.

"Santiago we have a problem."

He sighed. "We have a problem? Or you have a problem?"

"We."

Santiago blew air into the mouthpiece. "Meet me tomorrow at Maria's at noon," he said, before disconnecting the call.

"What are you going to do?" Keisha asked, rubbing my back.

I buried my face in my hands and groaned. "All I can do is tell him the truth and see what he says."

Chance

     I felt the same uncomfortable, un-welcoming vibe when I walked into Maria's for the first time almost a month ago. Santiago was sitting at the bar, sipping on a Budweiser, with a trusty security guard at his side. I swallowed my pride and fear at the same time as I headed over to the bar to join him.

     "So what is this problem we have?" Santiago asked, wasting no time about getting to the point.

     I fidgeted with my fingers as I stared at the countless bottles of liquor behind the bar. I couldn't look this man in the eye and tell him that I had fucked up.

     "Well...I was, uh...robbed last night."

     "What was that?" Santiago asked.

     "I was robbed last night. Motherfucker got me for everything."

     Santiago exhaled and shook his head. "I guess that is a problem." he said. "My precious product is in the hands of some hoodlum and you're short nearly four thousand."

     "Santiago, I swear—"

     "But it's no need to make this into a big deal. You just give me what you owe me and we're cool, amigo. There will be no bad blood between us," he explained.

I sighed and looked down at my hands. "He took me for everything. I don't know have a penny to my name."

Santiago groaned in frustration. "Okay. Now it's a big deal."

"I can"--

"I like you, Chance," he said, cutting me off. "So I am going to do you a favor."

I finally looked up at him. His gaze was intense, his expression serious. "I'm going to give you one day to come up with my money." He did some mental calculation in his head. "I'll settle with thirty-five hundred. That's pretty fair. You should be able to come up with that amount in a day. Right?"

"Um..."

"Right?" Santiago insisted.

"How am I supposed to come up with thirty-five hundred dollars?"

"Look I don't give a fuck how you come up with it, but you'd better. Because if you don't...I will kill you."

I quickly looked away.

"It's nothing personal. I understand you're a kid, but you must learn mistakes lead to consequences. I don't know if you were ever taught that, but I'm a strong believer in that."

I nodded my head.

"You can meet me tomorrow at the place where I do most of the drop offs?"

"At the docks."

He sighed. "Yes, Chance. At the docks." He said it as if he were speaking to a hardheaded two year old. "At nine." he added.

I stood up and headed out the door.

"Don't let me down, kid," he yelled after me.

Wisdom

I was in my dorm studying for an upcoming exam when my cell phone chirped its annoying ringtone. For two seconds, I debated if I should answer it. The ringing ceased after the fourth or fifth ring. Yet as soon I prepared to highlight a passage in my textbook, my cell phone began to chirp again.

I groaned as I slammed the highlighter down on my desk and answered the phone. "Hello", I answered in an agitated tone.

"Wisdom, it's me. Look, don't hang up!" Chance said breathlessly. "I'm in a fucked up situation now and I need you."

I snorted. "What else is new?"

"Yo, this ain't like the times in the past. I'm in some real deep shit. I...uh...I..."

"Spit it out, Chance!" I was growing more irritated by the moment by just hearing his voice.

"I owe this cat some money," he finally admitted. "And not some twenty dollars shit. I'm talking three thousand dollars!"

I sucked my teeth. "Three thousand dollars?"

He paused. "Well...thirty five hundred to be exact."

"Ask Johnny."

Chance remained silent for several seconds.
"Could you loan me the money?" he finally asked.

"Loan you?" I repeated sarcastically. "You mean
give you?"

"Come on, bro. Please!" Chance pleaded. "I can't
go to Aunt May and Uncle Lou. It's not even an option."

"Yeah. I know," I said flatly.

"So please, man. You gotta help me out. You gotta
come through for me."

"Well, actually I don't have to do a thing. You'll
have to get your own ass out of this mess."

"Wiz! Come on now, bro. You get college grant
money. I know about you sending Aunt May all that
fucking money. Why can't you look out for me this one
time?"

I was instantly offended that he would even bring
up such a thing. My grant money was my money to do
whatever with it that I pleased. If I chose to send Aunt
May money then that was my perogative. Not his
concern. I should have known he would throw something
so petty up in my face to make me feel guilty.

"I don't owe you shit, Chance!" I yelled, hoping I
made myself sound loud and clear.

"He said he's gonna kill me, bro!" Chance screamed, before bursting out crying into the phone.

I shook my head. "You know what? You're a real piece of work, Chance."

"Wiz, please!"

"I'm hanging up now"--

"He said he would kill Aunt May and Uncle Lou!" Chance blurted out.

I sighed, looked around my dorm room, and actually debated if I should help his selfish ass out or not.

"Why are you always dragging everyone else into your bullshit, Chance?" I asked him. "Why must people suffer because of your mistakes?"

Chance paused. "Mom, would've wanted you to be here for me no matter what," he said in a hoarse tone. "If you change your mind and decide to come through for me, I'll be at Susan's diner tomorrow from 6:30 to 8:30." With that said he disconnected the call.

Chance

"Did you talk to Wisdom," Keisha asked as soon as I walked into her apartment.

I sighed. "Yeah. He's not trying help me out." I sidestepped her and walked towards the refrigerator and pulled out a can of Colt 45. "Did you call your mother and ask her for the money?"

Keisha sighed. "She hung up on me the minute she heard my voice."

"Damn!" I yelled so loud that CJ started screaming and hollering.

Keisha's ran off to tend to CJ and I threw the can of beer at the cinder wall in a fit of rage. I kept replaying the impactive words Santiago had imprinted in my mind: You must learn mistakes lead to consequences.

***

"Hello?"

"Aunt May? It's Chance."

"How are you doing?"

"Rough."

She paused. "Why's that?"

"I'm messed up, Aunt May." I told her. "I'm in a bad situation and I really need some cash."

The phone line remained silent for an entire nerve-wrecking two minutes.

"I've been praying for you, Chance," she quietly said, before disconnecting the call.

"Aunt May?" I yelled into the phone even though I was well aware that she had hung up on me. Damn. Why was everyone turning their backs on me at a time when I needed them the most? Aunt May usually always had my back. She had bailed me out of jail on countless occasions and I was sure as hell she would come through for me now. Why was she treating me like she didn't give a damn about me? Three thousand dollars wasn't much to ask for. It was considered chump change to some people.

"Fuck!" I screamed as I hauled my cell phone at the cinder wall. My brick phone broke into pieces at the sudden impact. "Fuck!"

Wisdom

It was sad to admit that I had officially wiped my hands clean of my twin brother. I couldn't help him out this time. I was still hurt from what happened to Imani. And that pain alone had fueled my sudden hatred for him. He felt more like a distant cousin to me than a brother. How could a brother hurt you a in way that Chance had hurt me?

He had tainted my life with his bullshit. I could never look at him the same. I honestly didn't know if I held any love for him in my heart. Pity. Yes. But love...I couldn't say I felt any.

Yeah, I had the money to give him. And yeah, tomorrow was Saturday so I had a free day to ride down to Philly and give it to him if I wanted to. But I wasn't going to. My days of being my brother's keeper was over. He deserved whatever punishment he had coming.

<u>Chance</u>

I didn't get any sleep last night, and today's hours were rolling by quicker than ever. I needed more time to stall and sort out my options. But time wasn't on my side. And I had no more options to rely on.

"I have a little money saved up." Keisha said. "Not three thousand dollars but something. Maybe"--

"Keisha, I swear I'm done with this shit after this. This ain't no fucking way to live, bay. If somehow I get this money today to pay this cat back, I'm gonna tell him flat out, I'm done with this shit. Find another footman to pimp."

"You think Wisdom will come?"

I looked at the digital alarm clock. It read 4:26 p.m. "I hope so." I told her. "Let me get on this bus."

I climbed out of bed and pulled on a pair of jeans and a hoodie, and tucked my pistol in the back of my jeans.

"Chance!"

I turned around and looked at Keisha. There was so much concern and love in her eyes. "Be careful," she said. I made a silent promise to myself that after this shit was over I'd try my best never to dog or disrespect her again.

"I'll try."

"And come back," she added with tears in her
eyes.

I sighed. "Now that...I can't promise."

Chance

I waited for Wisdom to show up to Susan's Diner for an entire two hours. I knew he knew exactly where this place was. This used to be our mother's favorite spot to eat. Every Sunday after Church she used to bring us here and we'd all enjoy a banana split. Those were the good old days.

"Would you like another cup of water?" A heavy sat waitress behind the counter asked.

"No, I'm fine. I'm just waiting on someone. They should be here any minute." I had told her the exact same line an hour ago.

She grimaced as she wiped the space in front of me and removed my empty glass.

I believed he'd show up just as much as the waitress believed me. I didn't even know why I had persuaded myself that he'd come through for me knowing he'd made himself clear last night that he wasn't. I guessed a little part of me wanted to believe that he knew I was still his brother regardless of all the fucked up shit I had done to him.

I shook my head as I remembered a time when Wisdom had mistakenly been jumped by a gang of boys when we were fifteen. Of course they thought he was me. And even though I had witnessed it, I still ran off like a little bitch, lucky that it wasn't me.

"Yeah. He ain't coming." I told myself as I wiped a single tear away. "Why would he?"

I looked down at my reflection in the glass counter. I'd just have to tell Santiago I don't have his money. If he kills me then he kills me. Another tear quickly rolled down my cheek.

Suddenly, I saw a familiar reflection in the glass counter beside me. I looked up at Wisdom and wiped the tear away. "I know your punk ass wasn't up here crying. You knew I'd come through for you." He said, handing me a small manila envelope.

Before I accepted the money, I pulled him into a strong embrace and held him tightly as more tears had quickly escaped my eyes. The hug said all of the things I couldn't bring myself to say.

Wisdom patted me on the back. "Come on, man. Let's get this over with."

I wiped my nose with my sleeve. "Wisdom, I—"

He waved me off. "Don't. You don't have to." he said. "Uncle Lou was right. In the end we're all each other has."

Wisdom

"Is this where he wants you to meet him?" I asked Chance.

"Yeah."

"I don't know about this, Chance. This place is all secluded and shit. It just doesn't seem right." I said. "You trust this guy?"

"Wiz, he said if I give him his money I have nothing to worry about." Chance held up the manilla envelope. I have his money."

"Maybe I should go with you?" I told him

"I'll be fine," Chance insisted. "Just sit tight. This will be over soon."

I hated the way that sounded.

"Trust me," Chance assured me. "He's a man of money. As long as I got his money, I'm good."

I pulled across the street from the large abandoned brick building that stood adjacent to the docks.

"I'll be back. And thanks bro." Chance said before patting me on the shoulder. He departed the car and headed across the street to the building.

Chance

"You're six minutes late, Chance," Santiago said as I approached him. He was standing in the middle of his two bulky goons.

Although my heart was pounding like crazy, I tried to exuberate confidence. I had his money so I was good, right? Right?

"I'm sorry about that. But the good news is..." I produced the manilla envelope from my back pocket. "I have your money."

Santiago clasped his hands together. "See, that's good news for me." he paused. "There is no good news for you."

The smile on my face instantly turned into a frown. "What are you talking about?"

Santiago smiled. "Well, see, Chance...I've decided you're a loose end."

"What?"

"I don't think I want to take any more chances with you, Chance," he explained.

One of his goons snickered, but I didn't see a damn thing funny.

"It's time to tie up the loose end," Santiago continued. "I think it's best we sever ties."

One of his security guards pulled a polished black Glock from its holster and aimed it in my direction.

I held my hands up. "Wait! You don't have to do this! I have your money!" I yelled, as I waved the manilla envelope in their faces.

He shrugged his shoulders. "What can I say?" he asked. "Business is business."

The guard cocked the gun in my direction, but before he could pull the trigger, Wisdom smacked him upside the head with a steel pipe from behind.

His other security guard quickly reached for his gun, but before he could make his move I fired a single shot that landed in his temple.

Before Santiago could react I aimed my gun in his direction.

"Chance, you don't want to do this," he said putting his hands in the air.

"Oh, yeah. By the way...I quit," I said before squeezing the trigger.

Santiago suddenly burst into laughter at the realization that my gun was now empty. "You really fucked up, amigo," he said reaching for his gun.

Suddenly, Wisdom swung the steel pipe at his hand, knocking his weapon loose. Before Santiago could react, he slammed the pipe against his skull.

"Come on!" Wisdom yelled as Santiago hit the pavement."Let's get the fuck out of here!"

We both tore off running in the direction of Wisdom's car. I could see the faint hue of his white car-- Suddenly I heard a loud gunshot and felt a sharp pain in the back of my calf muscle. Several more gunshots rang through-out the night air.

I fell down instantly, and watched in horror as a gun pierced the center of Wisdom's back. He dropped a few feet from where I had been gunned down. I looked over my shoulder and noticed Santiago was slowly making his way over to us from afar.

I dragged myself over to Wisdom.

"Bro..."

Wisdom's entire shirt was drenched in blood. Dark red blood seeped from his mouth as he tried to force himself to look down at his wound.

I quickly wiped the blood away from his mouth. Tears were streaming down my cheeks as I lifted his head and held it my hands. I could hear the faint resonance of sirens approaching.

"Wisdom," I choked out.

"It's...it's okay," he said. His entire body was trembling and he was losing blood fast.

"Man, this ain't okay." I cried. "This shit ain't okay."

Wisdom held his hand up for me to take. I grabbed his bloodied hand and held onto it tightly.

"You know what?" Wisdom whispered.

"What?" I asked, as tears streamed down my cheeks.

Wisdom smiled. "I think that was me in the picture...with the snotty nose."

I smiled. "This ain't the time to be thinking about some shit like that," I told him.

His grip in my hand loosened. "This...is the perfect time," he whispered before his eyes became glazed over.

I softly closed his eyes as I rocked him in my arms like a newborn baby. Apart of me had just died. No. I had just died.

"Drop the fucking weapon!" I heard a cop scream in our direction.

I suddenly looked up and saw Santiago standing over me with blood oozing down the side of his face. His gun was aimed right at the top of my skull. Right about now I felt like begging him to pull the trigger.

Suddenly a cop fired a single shot that landed in his chest.

He dropped to ground on his knees and fell backwards.

"Chance!" Moretti yelled running up to my side. "Chance are you okay?" he asked.

I looked down at Wisdom.

"Hurry up. Give me the gun," he said, holding his hand out.

I looked down at the pistol, not even realizing that it was lying right beside me.

After I handed him the gun, he quickly wiped it off with his shirt and shoved it in the front of his jeans, before pulling his loose shirt over it. All the cops began rushing towards the scene.

"I'm sorry," Moretti whispered.

I looked down at my brother and touched the side of his warm face. "Yeah. So am I."

Chance

Four Days Later

"It's been a long...a long time coming...and I know...a change gone come. Oh. Yes it is!"" Aunt May cried tears of grief and sorrow as she sang Sam Cooke's "A Change is Gonna Come" at Wisdom's burial.

Uncle Lou rubbed me on the back as I cried like a baby at my brother's funeral. Rain pelted against face as tears streamed down my cheeks.

"Then I go...to my brother...And I say brother...help me please..."

I looked up and noticed Detective Moretti walking up towards the congregation. He nodded his head in my direction and I nodded mine in his.

Honestly, I didn't know what he did with that pistol, and truthfully I didn't care. The police never came knocking at my door and no one ever called questioning me. I didn't know why he did it for me. Maybe he felt sorry for me. I guess I'd never know.

After Aunt May finished singing her heartfelt a capella, the pastor asked the congregation if anyone would like to say a few words before the casket was lowered.

I wiped my nose with my sleeve and said, "I'd like to say something." Aunt May patted me on my back as I walked past her to the front of the congregation.

I cleared my throat. "Although...my brother and I sometimes didn't see eye to eye. He was..." I turned to face the casket. "You were my best friend, Wisdom." I wiped a tear away. "When I didn't believe in myself...you believed in me. When no one else is there for me...you'll always be in my corner...No matter what. And even though..." I paused, as pain overtook my senses. "Even though you might be gone in body. You're never gone in spirit. I love you, bro."

I let out a sigh of relief after I finished my speech, knowing my brother had heard that. I watched in sadness as his casket was lowered into the grave. Producing the same old, faded picture I had shown Imani, I looked it over. A smile tugged at the corner of my lips as I stared at Wisdom. I gently touched his face with my fingertips. Without deliberation I dropped it into his grave and headed back towards the congregation.

"Chance," Keisha said approaching me through the crowd of family and friends with CJ toted up on her hip.

<u>Chance</u>

2012

"Mr. Ainesworthe do you think I could get an extension on the assignment?" Tammy asked as my Psychology class departed.

"And why would I do that?" I asked as I straightened up the paperwork on my desk.

She leaned over her desk, revealing her bulging cleavage. Her little trick did next to nothing to impress a happily married man.

"Well, I'm having a hard time coming up with some ideas," she smiled.

I sighed. "I'm afraid I can't do that Ms. Hanes. If I choose to make one stipulation for you, then I'll be forced to do the same for the entire class. Now the deadline is January 21st. If you can't come up with a plausible paper by then, then I don't know what to tell you."

She sulked and made a face before she stomped out of the classroom.

"Dad, can I use the car?" CJ asked approaching my desk. "Me and some of the guys are going to go hang out."

"Hang out?" I repeated as I removed my reading glasses.

He shrugged his shoulders. "Yeah. Hang out."

"Remember you're not twenty-one for another two weeks."

CJ sucked his teeth. "So? What is that supposed to mean?"

"Do you really have to ask?"

"You have my word. I won't drink and drive."

I hesitantly pulled out my car keys and tossed them to him.

"I wonder how many girl's numbers I can get driving a Prius?" he joked.

"Hey!" I held up a finger. "You can always walk or catch the bus."

He began jingling the keys. "Naw. I'll take this alternative."

Chance

It actually was a nice day to walk. I could've called my wife to pick me up, but today I felt like enjoying the weather. Besides, I only lived a few blocks from where I taught at Philadelphia University. However, I wasn't planning on going home.

One bus ride later I found myself walking through Indigo Cemetery. I stopped once I reached Wisdom's grave site. His grave stood right beside our mother's.

"Filthy," I complained as I began pulling the weeds from around their tombstones.

After I was satisfied that both of their grave sites looked a little more appealing, I stole the fresh bouquet of flowers laid against the tombstone beside my mother's grave.

"Sorry Helen," I said as I split the bouquet of flowers into two separate bunches. I laid half of the flowers against my mother's tombstone and the other against my brothers.

I shook my head and laughed to myself. "I guess some habits die hard, huh, bro?"

THE END

Excerpt from "Ebony and Ivory"

Mario reclined his head as he allowed nature to take its course...Suddenly, the sound of movement startled him. He assumed Ebony had just come into the bathroom behind him. The minute he turned and looked behind himself, he flinched at the unexpected sight of the woman standing beside the doorframe with her back pressed against the wall. He had walked right past her and not even noticed her. Subconsciously, he released his dick and his urine spilled onto the toilet seat before spraying the white tile surrounding his feet.

"What the...fuck?" Mario looked to Ivory then back at Ebony who was sitting up in bed with the sheets nestled tightly around her bosom. Their expressions matched, and it wasn't simply because they were identical twins. They were in cahoots with one another! It took Mario less than two seconds to realize what was going on. "You bitches tryin' to rob me?!"

There was a tense moment of silence before anyone spoke again. Ebony's heart beat rapidly as her fists clutched the plush sheets. Ivory's chest heaved up and down slowly as she took uneven breaths. Her eyes darted in every direction but she refused to look at Mario.

I knew I shouldn't have let Ebony's ass talk me into this shit, Ivory thought. If we make it out of here, I will never do anything like this again, she promised herself.

Ebony was the first to break the nerve-racking silence. "M—Mario," she stuttered. "Let me explain..."

Ivory however wasn't trying to explain a damn thing. She just wanted to get out of this situation by any means necessary. In a sudden state of panic and fear she darted towards the bathroom door in order to flee—

Yet Mario's fist instantly caught hold of her quick weave, halting her in her tracks.

"Aaahh!" she cried out in pain.

Her tear ducts stung as she felt small strands of her real hair being torn from her scalp underneath the quick weave. If she could, she would have gladly taken off running, leaving the eighteen inch weave in his tight grip. Yet the fresh quick weave was done far too tightly to permit her escape.

"And where the fuck you think you goin' hoe?!" he sneered.

Ebony quickly jumped out the bed butt ass naked at the exact same moment that Mario slammed Ivory's skull against the doorframe.

"Don't touch her motherfucker!" Ebony screamed. Spittle flew from her mouth as she yelled and charged at him full speed.

Ivory's limp body went crashing into the bathroom tile. Ebony was unsure if she was either conscious or out cold. Cocking her fist back, she ran towards Mario and took an uncoordinated swing towards his head.

He quickly and effortlessly ducked her futile blow before sending a vicious slap across her left cheek. Ebony went flying backwards before falling against the bathroom's marble wall. Her head collided with the wall upon impact and she uncontrollably slid down onto the floor. Dark red blood leaked from the split in her bottom lip, dripping down her chin.

"Ya'll hoes got the right one!" he yelled cockily.

The minute he knocked one sister down, the other one had managed to get back to her feet. Without warning, Ivory jumped onto Mario's back and locked both arms tightly around his neck. She screamed like a madwoman while struggling to cause damage to the six foot two inch two hundred and ten pound man.

Her head was throbbing like hell and there was even a small speed knot that had quickly formed in the center of her forehead. Yet she was determined to fight back.

Mario spent around in half circles, desperately trying to pull Ivory off his back. The minute he grabbed a fistful of her hair, he gave it a powerful tug and snatched her onto the floor. Before she was able to recuperate, he sent a devastating blow to her right jaw.

Her entire jawbone shook from the force of the unexpected punch and she feared he might have actually broken it.

"Aaaaahhhhh!" Ebony came up from behind Mario screaming like a woman possessed. Suddenly the ceramic soap dish that was clutched tightly in her left hand came crashing down onto Mario's bald head.

"Aahh! Shit!" he yelled, keeling over in pain.

The soap dish broke into several pieces upon impact. Ebony assumed the blow would have knocked him unconscious but she was disappointed that it only caused him to stagger. With the single small shard that was left in her hand, Ebony sliced the back of Mario's neck.

"Fuck!" he cried out in pain before clamping his hand over the semi-deep gash.

Both sisters didn't give him a chance to retaliate as they proceeded to punch, kick, and stomp their target. Even with all the simultaneous blows being inflicted upon him, Mario wouldn't go down so easily.

ABOUT THE AUTHOR

Jade Jones discovered her passion for creative writing in elementary school. Born in 1989, she began writing poetry as an outlet. She then converted her poetry into short stories and started using her life experiences to create characters. Jade fell in love with the art and used storytelling as a means of venting.

Jade currently resides in Atlanta, Georgia. With no children, she spends her leisure shopping and traveling. She says that seeing new faces, meeting new people, and experiencing diverse cultures fuels her creativity. The stories are generated in her heart, the craft is practiced in her mind, and she expresses her passion through ink.

If you have any questions or would like to interact please add her on Facebook at: Author Jade Jones or follow her on Instagram and Twitter @Jade_Jones89.

OTHER JADED
PUBLICATIONS TITLES

Tales from da 216

Nobody's Perfect Angel

My Brother's Keeper

Cameron

Cameron 2

Cameron 3

Cameron 4

Love's Triangle

Ghetto Pocahontas Uncut

Femme Fatale: Passion Comes with a Price

Backpage

No Good Spouses

Schemin'

Still Schemin'

Stay Schemin'

CPSIA information can be obtained
at www.ICGtesting.com
Printed in the USA
LVOW13s2018020317

525948LV00013B/1474/P